THE ALPHABET TAX

THE ALPHABET TAX

ROSA WOOLF AINLEY

grand IOTA

Published by
grandIOTA

2 Shoreline, St Margaret's Rd, St Leonards TN37 6FB
&
37 Downsway, North Woodingdean, Brighton BN2 6BD

www.grandiota.co.uk

First edition 2023
Typesetting & book design by Reality Street
Title page image: © Raimond Spekking / CC BY-SA 4.0
(via Wikimedia Commons), detail

A catalogue record for this book is available from the British Library

ISBN: 978-1-874400-88-2

Contents

" 'Ave to teach you the ABC next."

– George Orwell, *1984*

Glossary of useful terms for archive users

Alfabs/alfabettis – an unofficial self-defining term among those receiving benefit; also used by Coders; see also Delites, Gifted, Recips, Units

AlphaCode – shortened title of the regime's full AlphaCode Conversion (original discontinued version: AlphaSyntax); ACode used by archive group and others in the postCode era

Delites – shortened version of "deliterati", a slang term from the early days used by those receiving benefit; and by Coders; see also Alfabs, Gifted, Recips, Units

Delivery dogs – disparaging term used by their superiors for AlphaCode workers; otherwise known as operatives or trustees (see below)

Full-hander – those in receipt of complete alphabet, the 26 letters; see also Two-hander/Three-hander

Gifted – those in receipt of benefit (official term); see also Alfabs, Delites, Recips, Units

Literati – those above and beyond the remit of the Code, with all the letters and no prospect of benefit being granted

Operative – those in low-grade positions delivering the AlphaCode; see also Delivery dogs

Recovered – those with all letters withdrawn; in official parlance, those in receipt of full benefit

Recips – short for recipients, a vernacular term established and used by Trustees/Operatives then banned by the AlphaCode Executive Ministry

Scrabble – the exclamation once full recovery is reached, as in "It's a Scrabble"; see also Alfabs, Delites, Gifted, Recips, Units

Trustee – another term for those in low-grade positions delivering the AlphaCode

Two-hander/Three-hander – among those receiving benefit, refers to number of letters allocated; two-hander=10, three-hander=15; in official parlance this would be referred to as "benefit levels"; see also Full-hander

Units – people in receipt of benefit; see also Alfabs, Delites, Gifted, Recips

Wall-Es, aka Wallys – the resistance, those who set up letterbanks, among other initiatives

Watcher/watchman – street-level enforcement troop established for early AlphaCode implementation; later stepped back to office-level operation

Keynote[1]

"Welcome to Central House/s, historic home of the great AlphaCode Conversion. So glad you could attend this conference for all us like-minded AlphaCoders.

"To begin a presentation with a provocation has long been the norm. But enough of that! Ever at the forefront of change, we are doing things differently. There's simply no need for that kind of incitement when we have, as we do, the pleasure of consensus. We are united in our resolve to upgrade and implement the newly transformed Code right across the board. I don't need to remind you that we were brought to this point by The Hardship. I suspect none of you need to hear more about that. So let's not pick over those depressing bones any more than we have to. Everyone accepts that many units struggle with meeting their goals because of being over-encumbered with choice. They cannot cope with their letter load. The level of expectation that comes with access to so many letters is too much for them to cope with. They need help with this; always did. That's why we are here.

"But before we get down to the current whys and wherefores, let me rewind a little for those of you who have joined us more recently, new recruits to our stalwart band of believers. I will lay out in the simplest possible terms what the AlphaCode Conversion means, what we have done, and what we are now implementing to complete our journey. And that's not just for our new members. Due to our immersion in day-to-day delivery, it is all too easy to forget how we

1 Note that additional information for the print version is added here in bold type [not to be included in spoken delivery].

got here in the first place: the long-shared belief of us Coders that units had no right to sully our precious space with their noise.

"Among this trusted cohort of Coders, straight talking is required, so here goes. The AlphaCode was designed to fix one of society's more disturbing and enduring problems: the clamour of dissent and violent counter-opinion. Too many hurtful, aggressive shouters, in many cases transgressing, if not our laws, then codes of shared acceptable behaviour. Every word uttered, every syllable, has a cost. We can no longer afford to put up with incessant complaints from the units. Nor should we.

"We must acknowledge that not everyone subscribes to our vision of a calm and pleasant future, but our aim is and always has been peaceful, co-operative coexistence. Freeing the units from the need to use vocabulary outside their lexical comfort zone is of paramount importance. They struggle with all-but-incomprehensible rules of spelling, grammar and syntax, so expecting them to engage in complex discourse is unrealistic and unfair. It was obvious that their skills and energy could best be utilised in other ways. Evenhandedness is beside the point. Providing a more appropriate distribution of resources, advantageous both to giver and receiver, is what needed to be implemented.

"That's where The AlphaCode Conversion came in. Many years ago, after The Hardship, we had a choice to make: descend further to a baseline incalculably low, of which we could not conceive, or build on it. We chose the latter, using it as the foundation for the righting of innumerable social wrongs and for, of course, the greater good. While all eyes were on The Hardship and all ears on The Quiet, it was exactly the right time to institute our long-dreamed-of Conversion. We took our chance, seized the day.

"For the wellbeing of all concerned – the entire population, across all social strata – a decision was made to intervene, to curb the mistaken belief that people could say whatever they wanted, wherever and whenever and to whomever they wanted, and that it was their right and privilege to do so. The privilege, if I may be so bold, was ours alone. We had to act decisively, while we could, to take advantage of what we feared was the briefest window of opportunity, in case the end of The Hardship brought about a return to the old normal, when everyone expressed themselves as loudly as possible whenever they felt like it. Happily, we were mistaken about The Hardship. It was a deeper recession than expected, and we grabbed the opportunity it presented for us.

"When the first phase of the shutdown – the month of Big Quiet, as it became known – was announced during The Hardship, cue much weeping and wailing, as well as the usual blather about civil rights and the need to communicate with loved ones. Which completely missed the point, of course. Simples: no talking. None. We had to have peace and quiet as a national safeguard; and we also needed space and time to decide what to do next. How to break the stalemate. How to stem the ever-increasing flow of lies and falsehood. Because we had a lot to try to achieve in our month of peace and quiet, people were allowed to leave their safe bubbles of silence for only one hour per day.

[next slide please]

"By then the Conversion system was up and running. The levels of compliance were fairly good, but the non-compliance led us to extend the rule of silence. First to three months, then six more, followed by 'maybe next year or the year after', until it had been pushed so far into the future there was no need to announce it any more. The Big Quiet was where we are and what we do. The AlphaCode Conversion is what we turned it into from thereon: our Ministry. We turned silence into benefit – that was the nature of the Conversion. It maximised the austerity assets of The Hardship and extended them for the general good.

"Initially, to stop particular topics – war, revolution, rights, freedom – being discussed, we placed a ban on certain words. These words – too many to mention here, but I'm sure you get the drift – couldn't be used on pain of unspecified sanctions and/or fines.[2] The policing of thought began by policing language: what was heard and what was said. But the ban imposed on the use of certain words was merely the starting point. Units had to be made to get to grips with the idea that they couldn't spout willy-nilly whatever arrant nonsense came into their heads, though many of them held the strange belief that they could. And although the ban worked well enough, we soon came to the realisation that in and of itself it wasn't sufficient, that we had to do something more. But what?

"Because words lay at the root of the problem, we realised that by limiting access to certain letters, the units would be obliged, for once, to 'think' before speaking, as in 'Do I have the letters to say that?', thus considerably reducing noise and increasing the quiet. By such means we saw that we could restructure society and rebuild it anew, piece by piece, letter by letter, for the betterment of all.[3]

"What I now want to address is the 'how' on the ground, by which I mean the system of implementation.

2 Such rules were applied solely to units, or the "deliterati", as they came to be known among ourselves. Note to self: "Delites", "Deliterati" – outmoded and inaccurate terminology. Do not use!

3 For full reports on concept, strategy, sanctions, evaluation, comms, and safety procedures, please look up the relevant papers.

"The system used to revolve around an abidance mechanism, a set of structures through which those enabled to participate – the Gifted, as they're known – would demonstrate their wholehearted commitment to the standards and rules they'd agreed to as part of their adherence to the benefit programme. Many of the units are compliant in helping us to achieve this goal, and that is to be commended. For those who are, for whatever reason, non-compliant, to bring them to this understanding is a longer-term undertaking on our part. Their benefits will reflect this.

"You have also been told that this worked effectively through the use of benefit cards and letter allocation books, and in its time it did. Each unit was subject to constant checks and balances. They had to sign in at a particular time and place to receive that month's allocation or stipend. If they failed in this simple task, their benefit levels would be impacted negatively. Overall we succeeded, more quickly than we thought possible, in embedding in the population an awareness of the dangers of over-speaking. Bluntly put: Keep quiet or else! Soon we introduced new militias for these times – the AlphaWatch and their backup, the 'local influence force', aka snitchers. Their job was to report on the misuse of letters and to undertake loudness patrols. The thrust of our work then shifted to compliance enforcement, which is precisely what we're building on now.

"The Conversion seeks to embed in society an entirely new form of positive discrimination. Such an extensive change is bound to take time to implement. Nonetheless, the full effects were predictable from the outset, and early signs were consistently excellent. The multiplicity of quick wins and unexpected benefits (the title of one of this afternoon's in-depth sessions, by the way; please do sign up for it) includes the work of the so-called 'influencers', a legion of units prepared – indeed, often desperately enthusiastic! –

to inform on the actual and supposed misdeeds of their neighbours. Another unexpected benefit was the motivational power of fear, which proved more effective than any sanction imposed by the Code. The red feather of silence was another important tool we introduced. Though randomly applied and actually powerless, it served to remind recipients that their benefit was spent and it scared them into submission.

"The beauty of the design, structure and delivery of this programme, of which we are justifiably proud, is the simultaneous giving and saving across the units. Each unit has its needs attended to by being given, for example, guidance about which letters to avoid in order to steer clear of extra difficulty. As is obvious to one and all, giving is at the heart of what we do! But there's no question among the units of voluntary decision or choice. The letters are of limited availability and not all needs can be met. They must manage as best they can with what they're given.

[next slide please]

"Benefits – letter provision, to be clear – are set at the ideal level for each unit, pitched just right at their assessed level of conversation delivery needs. Individual ~~rations~~ allowances are predicated on local and regional averages. Benefit is carefully calibrated to fit the applicant's needs for that specific time period. To reiterate: Everyone has what they need, leaving them more fully in accord with their potential. The ensuing system brings improved – it might not be too strong to say perfect – communication, and this involves both giving and taking, participation and implementation.

[next slide, please: See also:
'The New Age of Disclosure and Spreading']

"This arrangement is also among the breadth of advantages across the different levels of beneficiaries – those in recovery and those still in the early stages. All of them we term Gifted because, it hardly needs saying, the benefit is an absolute gift to them. It's also a 'gift' to the rest of us. Get your head around this: they get more benefit where needed. And more benefit – well, that means fewer letters! Always lightening the load, that's us, what we do. The complete absence of complaint, question or protest demonstrates the worth and success of the benefit system. Not a murmur, not a cavil.[4] In such a perfect situation, no agreement is necessary. It's a given.

"Put another way: relaxing demands on units by removing the pressures of too many letters places them on The Road to Recovery, the official over-arching term for our programme.[5] We make everything better for them until they reach a state of total recovery. Recovery is the end point of the re-evaluation process, undertaken by every applicant. This is expensive, granted, but the greater the number of units that can be brought to recovery the better. It is highly cost-effective.

"Our response to the need for change went to the very root of the problem, as you have heard: to the letters themselves. Getting to this gritty level of detail is a major achievement. Honouring the truth of AlphaCode Conversion can mean tough love, though I must emphasise that these ideas were modified slightly for public consumption – the units need not be troubled by either the philosophy or the theoretical grounding of AlphaCode, just the requirements.

---

4 Sanctions against complaint remain fully operational.

5 **Too much detail here?** ~~Demands on the Gifted are well documented.~~ It is precisely these that the system is alleviating so thoroughly. Demand is now much more widely acknowledged in its effects on resources. ~~This is still a relatively new area for research and although publicly – within governmental directives – the programme is complete, there always remains considerable work to be done.~~

"The Conversion was absolutely the right thing to do, therefore there is nothing to be gained by postponing this extension to Code enforcement or introducing it in piecemeal fashion. Have no doubt: making a total change in one fell swoop is both highly cost-effective and more productive. Which is exactly what we wish to achieve. Our system, as it were, 'washes its own face'. And that our approach has changed over time indicates the advanced, forward-thinking nature of the Code. Not for us a limited tinkering-at-the-edges review! Not for us a namby-pamby trial roll-out in the back of beyond! For safety's sake we must close down all avenues of expression. Our planning at this level is now complete.[6]

"On to our next steps. We have to acknowledge that we were wasting resources. Time was being spent unnecessarily, not least by ourselves, but also by our watchers, in reporting on noise levels and word use at street level. Change was required. The watchers have since been upgraded and given trustee status, partly as a time-saving measure, but also because it became obvious that such an effective and successful system as this works without compulsion – sticks, carrots and threats simply weren't required. We have further embraced the creative possibilities of new technology. Listening devices recently installed in interior and exterior spaces are having the desired effect. We are fast-forwarding the future our work was designed to create.

"You may be surprised to hear that units are constantly finding new ways to disseminate their annoying squeaks and squawks. There are those who think they know better than we do and never give up. Hence we constantly re-evaluate our processes, to counter their changing ways with our own. New forms of surveillance include ones that provide

6 **Subject to annual review.**

valuable sources of information for us, as one would expect. But, perhaps best of all, there are some that enforce unit compliance while delivering nothing, absolutely nothing, relieving us of having to deal with yet more dreary data. There's always more work to be done, another mountain to climb, new forms of revolt to be dealt with, but, that said, the freshly implemented mechanisms of the Code are primed to deal with much of this.

[next slide please]

"Very soon, the recruitment of an entirely new staff cohort is scheduled to begin. Having gone through the rigorous training process, the new trustees will implement delivery in innovative ways that will be smoother, less bureaucratic, and more useful to all those involved, bringing hope and security to the beneficiaries. Staff members will be selected for their appropriateness to receive specific training in how to deliver the updated strategy. To spread the benefits even further, they will receive this training free of charge.[7]

"Soon we will be ready to unveil our Central House/s portfolio: locations specially adapted to welcome benefit recipients and respond to individual needs. This is an exciting project, exploring new ways of using old buildings. The rehabilitation programme will be undertaken alongside the reform of the system. Indeed, the buildings constitute a significant part of the new system, and the architectural work is imminent – watch this space! Our extensive portfolio makes clear the breadth of application of our investment, and we are confident of success. Together with the aforementioned training provision, it is designed to maximise

---

7 **In case of questions, remember, this is tbc.** It will probably work through a process of reimbursement once training is completed and the probation period successfully discharged. Details of charges for office space, rental and uniforms will be set; **also tbc.**

economy across physical premises and extensive refits, facilitating a roll-out of completely redesigned systems machinery and administrative materials.

"Needless to say, we still have to ensure that no unit is abusing our generously allocated resources. One of the defining principles of the new Code is to keep our focus onward and upward. Our over-arching aim is to aid those in benefit, enabling them to move on to new life paths in their recovering state and live happy, healthy, meaningful lives in the premises specially redeveloped for them. Anything that deviates from this goal will be dealt with swiftly and with no half-measures.

"The restructured benefit system will soon be seen as a welcome release from the demands of service, a lightening of the terms of contract, allowing any entitled unit the privilege of silence and the ability to step back from the exigencies of full-time engagement. Equitable, nimble and forward-looking, as indeed we are, we are confident that the new Code will be heralded for decades to come as an outstanding solution to the disarray of language use and the violent loudness foisted on us all. This is a customised creative fix for these times, and our expectation is that this form of governmental innovation will soon be in demand across national boundaries. In today's sessions you will hear about this and other aspects of the system, including the buildings, recruitment plans, sanctions and, as mentioned, those unexpected extras already identified.

"Care is, of course, the cornerstone of our work, and our hearts go out to those units who need more support. But progress must continue apace. This new initiative will bring about a clearer, fairer system. The Conversion strategy is a radical policy based on recasting the knowledge amassed by our colleagues from the highest echelons of business, science, government, and the research community. Because of their invaluable work, we are in the fortunate position of knowing that the Conversion strategy will bring about the desired result: a shared and peaceful future for all.

[next slide please]

"This is about so much more than replacing a moribund, unwieldy system with a near-version of itself that will quickly become outmoded and dysfunctional. It is much more than a system, even; it is an ethos.[8] Naturally, we find self-congratulation distasteful and somewhat embarrassing, but there is no doubt that we are presiding over the fullest root-and-branch reform of social interaction standards in recorded history, and success is guaranteed. Recognition of the enormous impact of this work, and our role in it, will surely come; but now is not the time for celebration. We must ensure that the development from policy to implementation is actioned swiftly and executed with the same degree of managerial acumen, accuracy and speed as concept is to strategy and strategy to protocol.

"Going forward (as we do, always), we believe it is our obligation, as people who know instinctively how to communicate in an appropriate manner, to spread such good fortune to the units. But it has not been easy. For the sake of progress we've had to make sacrifices and take on many new responsibilities. We are in perpetual stewardship of our wealth of resources – and I'm referring here not only to our guardianship of language but also to our new hosting premises, Central House/s. The writing is on the wall – or rather, walls. Because our principal duty, onerous but joy-

---

8 **See above comment. Depending on prior knowledge of participants, add:** "There are those for whom it has become almost a religion." This is not to be encouraged. It displays, if anything, a lack of understanding of our position as AlphaCode Ministry.

fully borne, is to those less fortunate than ourselves, we will continue to persevere with the system updates I have outlined today. We watch and fully utilise all emergent forms. Our mission is to remedy wrongs, now and always.

"Even without scanning your faces for confirmation, I can tell what you're thinking. 'Amazing, isn't it? Too much to hope for.' I say to you all: Yes, it is amazing. We can do it all through this new system. And once it becomes apparent how perfectly the system works for each and every unit, its generosity will be universally acclaimed.

"I say again, 'Welcome, this is the AlphaCode Conversion.' There will now be a short period for questions.

•

"No questions? Okay. Let's talk over refreshments!"

[slide: 'Bringing about Positive, Permanent Shifts in the Quality of Your Life and Peace of Mind for Your Future']

[end keynote]

From the Archivists

About Us

Let's start at the beginning. We are a self-organised, informal, untrained and unofficial group of laypeople who have come together to do the best we can to construct an archive. Each member of the archive group has added their voice to this introduction, as well as to this publication and to the project as a whole. It is therefore a collective enterprise, not one of individual ambition, and we have chosen to remain anonymous as there still remain fears of reprisals from the Taxers (which is what we call the AlphaCoders) and their cohort. More about them later.

What we have to do now is make decisions about our collective future after this appalling chapter in our history under the Alpha-Code regime. We have to make amends too. We must strive to discover what happened to us and how, what we allowed to happen and to what extent we were culpable. At every level and in every dimension, from individual to family, neighbourhood to nation, from active engagement to complicity and wilful ignorance, from victimhood to survivor status, questions must be answered.

The archive is formed of two parts, the first of which is a public record of the evil – not too strong a word, we think – work of the Coders, providing access to documents found in their HQs, known as Central Houses, that are dotted throughout the country. The archive's other part is about us, by which we mean all of us who lived under the oppressive yoke of the Taxers' AlphaCode (or ACode as we have started to call it). It's about making a record of our stories, not only looking back to the horror of what we lived through under their twisted regime, but also looking forward with hope, to what might be possible. We must ensure that nothing like the ACode happens again. We move tentatively towards the after-Tax, the deconversion, into the PostCode era. We consider what it might look like, or, better still, how we might make it look. To do so we are obliged to revisit that past, but with a degree of caution. Our hope is that the archive and this publication will make small steps in that direction, to guide us to better times.

Our stories, individual and collective, though painful in various ways and to different degrees, are of vital importance and must be heard. We want to offer friendly, non-adversarial settings in which those who attend our meetings are not only free to speak but also to contribute to the archive and to any documents we decide to publish. What part of your story you want to tell and how you want to tell it is your choice alone, always – don't let anyone tell you any different. You talk, and what you say is recorded and placed in the archive holdings, with or without your name, as you wish. For all of us, the citizens of this country, talking and sharing our stories is one way forward PostCode. How that's going to be made possible, given that there are those of us who cannot speak at all, and many more still in the process of tentatively emerging from the AlphaCode, we don't yet know.

These pages include both parts of the archive. They contain a curated selection of ACode paperwork, along with stories and interviews from our side. We weren't sure what to do with the rest of the ACode material. Burn it? That's what some of us wanted. "Burn the lot! Destroy it, like they tried to destroy us!" Such anger is understandable. Others in the group wanted to keep it all in perpetuity, to make a huge house for it, some kind of museum or library, turning it into something that will help us make new memories. But reading that material may not be enough. Perhaps we should open up the Central Houses, especially the top floors where the Taxers worked and looked down on us, so everyone can see what was going on. And anyway, it has to be acknowledged that reading, or the inability to do so, is an ongoing problem; it may take a good long while to bring that skill back into common use. In the meantime, if people can't read, those of us who can will read to them in our open-house meetings.

For your safety and wellbeing we are limiting the material that can be accessed in the archive, just until we've decided how much of the ACode material to keep and where to keep it. In the following pages we present a small range of material: documents, manifestos, treatises, etc. We urge readers not to underestimate the potential risk to their mental health when dealing with this material. Approach with caution. However much we may want it to go away, that can't and will not happen.

Positivity alert: in the coming months, as an additional means of crafting a new future for us all, we archivers will lay out our proposals for group healing sessions.

About the Code

The documentary material left in Central Houses, some of which is reproduced here, leaves us in no doubt what the AlphaCoders did, though it's almost impossible to explain their whys and wherefores, their whats and hows. Their documents can, however, show what led up to and informed the ACoders' power grab, principally how they used the Conversion to silence us all. During the time of The Hardship, those who were unable to support or care for themselves quadrupled in number. It was a bewildering and frightening time (but satisfying for some, it transpired). Basically, The Hardship provided the context for the Taxers-to-be to stake their claim and implement their programme.

Programme – that's what they called it. Or strategy, thesis, system, mechanism, or ... whatever. But no matter what it was called, it amounted to nothing. Their precious system, the Conversion, was all smoke and mirrors. There was no system, only the illusion of one, played out with multiple characters on numerous stages.

Although the whole thing was cobbled together out of ill-fitting parts, it still sufficed to turn society upside down and wreak havoc.

The Hardship brought about unprecedented levels of insecurity. It spanned all classes and professions and hit us, every one of us, hard. It was the age's major catastrophe. Then the watchers arrived, a veritable militia. In turn, the watchers co-opted some of those most badly hit by The Hardship. There were two levels of Coder troops back then: the watchers and their snitchers. The former signed up in their millions – not that they had much choice really – but they took to the work with enthusiasm. Suddenly they were all over the streets, absolutely everywhere, keeping us indoors and anxious during the shutdowns. They ensured we were quiet on our way to Central and that we knew there wasn't anywhere else for us to go. That, in a nutshell, is how the Code took root.

What kept us on our toes wasn't just the watchers. There was also a cohort of snitchers, informants who seemed happy to betray friends, family and neighbours they suspected of saying too much. And then there were the techies, ordered to make us believe they were fitting sensitive recording equipment in our homes. Between them and the Quiet, it was enough to make everyone nervous. How easily we were cowed by these tactics horrifies us to this day.

Let's be clear, the Code made absolutely no sense. It didn't function in the way they said it did. What the Coders touted as a world-beating system, supported on the ground by their militias, was a sham, a lie. But, catastrophically for us, it worked all too well.

Some watcher and snitcher testimony is available to be read in the archive, but there's nothing from the pretend techies, not a single story. That's because we've never come across even one of them. We know that many watchers came to a sticky end, so it's likely that once the techies had installed the kit that was never actually

meant to work they too were "disappeared". That's Coder grati-
tude for you: both watchers and techies contributed significantly to
establishing the Coders' regime, and then, when it was done, presumably they were deemed surplus to requirements.

What we do know is that people were so shattered by The Hardship they – we, most of us – rolled over in response to ATax after
the shutdowns, post-Hardship. "Something has to be done" was
the general sentiment, "and perhaps this will work. We've got to
pull together." Frankly, we were too desperate to discuss the matter sensibly. "Catastrophe fatigue" some have called it. Already
scared, not knowing what to do for the best, we simply allowed it
to happen. We let ourselves be ushered into the first round of
shutdown, the so-called Big Quiet. We didn't stand up to or against
the rest of it either. It began simply enough with curfews: 6 to 6,
with key exceptions. Then, before we knew what was what, we
were allowed out for only an hour a day. You had to book a slot
and show your pass. Then it was the quiets and benefits and allocations. And the watchers. The Centrals. The works, in other words.
Soon we were spending nearly all our time thinking about how we
could say what we had to say in the fewest letters possible, in case
we got caught out by the watchers, and too scared to think of how
to get our letters back. They made out it was our duty, and their
programme was going to help us. And we fell for it.

We certainly fell for the "We Hear You" line. As though they
cared about how we felt and were keen to help us through whatever difficulties had arisen. By the time "We Hear YOU" appeared
on signs that were posted everywhere, in every public space and
building, it was too late. We'd taken the bait and the Coders had
taken over.

What is unquestionable is that their Code, Tax, Conversion, whatever you wish to call it, doesn't add up. It's like they never even
thought it through. The examples we've chosen to share make
that plain. If the Taxers had been successful in getting all of us off

the streets and silent, completely silent (100 per cent recovery, as they saw it), what would the consequences have been? How would the economy function? Who, for instance, would do all the work, the low-grade but essential stuff, and a million other jobs besides? Society would be brought to the brink of collapse and there'd be no one to blame but the Coders themselves. Were they so privileged and smug that they believed they had a handle on chance, that it would all somehow turn out right? But in the end they knew to scarper while the going was good. Even if they didn't recognise how despicable and wrong the ATax was, they realised when it was over.

About Them

Although delivered to a cohort of true believers, the conference keynote you've just read by the anonymous ACode leader tells us very little about the awful truths of the, as they called it, Alpha-Code Conversion (as though it were some kind of religious experience, which undoubtedly to some of them it was). We who suffered so much under their rule call it the Alphabet Tax, for reasons that will soon become clear. The speech tells you nothing about the authoritarian nature of their power grab and the abusive practices it fostered. Publicly, in documents like this keynote, they glossed over their aims and the means by which they executed them. All of it was designed to ensure that only their ideas, opinions and voices were heard.

They certainly weren't giving themselves away. Not a bit of it. No one knows who wrote the reports, strategies and memos gathered here for you to read. No names, only initials, and only in a few places at that. Some of the documents we've uncovered contain comments and notes, also anonymous, in other hands. Clearly, they revised their documents time and time again, and because most were undated there's often a degree of confusion as to which one came first and which, if any, is the definitive statement. So much for their "rigorous system"! On some pages they say their work is complete and they've successfully transformed the world, hurrah. On others it's still a work in progress. And everything is on paper – no devices, no sticks, no drives, nothing like that. Who knows what they did with the computers. All gone. There were huge piles of ash, too, in the Central Houses. You have to wonder what it was they were burning given the incriminating material they left behind.

In what we've found so far there is little information about many of the enforcement procedures they trialled or established. Some we know about from our own experience. But apart from the stamp books and the various forms of the red feather, very few of these procedures were actioned. They simply weren't needed. The brigades and forces, the branding and codes, the chips and implants, the pharmaceuticals, surgical procedures, and probably much else, were never deployed. If studies were undertaken to investigate whether these methods would be effective, we've yet to find them. Most likely they've been reduced to ashes, among the first things to go.

About the Report

As for an explanation – as though anything could ever truly explain the Tax – the following report is the best of the documents we've discovered so far. We acknowledge that there are still omissions and uncertainties. Many of our fellow archivists suspect that's how things are likely to remain. It doesn't all add up – we know that. And while we apologise for not being able to connect all the dots, the deeper we delve into the AlphaCode paper trail, the more we become convinced that much of their so-called perfect system existed not on paper but only in the heads of those responsible for creating it.

From the tone of the documents collected here, we suspect the Coders retained them because they thought, perhaps genuinely believed, they were doing good, improving lives, making a valuable contribution to society. How seduced they were by their own power. Or perhaps they just wanted to gloat about how easily they'd manufactured consent and how their ATax system became the new normal, accepted, admired, perhaps even envied by other authoritarians who didn't have the courage of their convictions, and no one dared say a word against it. No one could, that's the thing.

To reiterate, this report is a collection of examples of archival deposits, including both found Coder materials and excerpts from recent conversation forums and interviews we have arranged and participated in. The aim is to try to build a picture of what happened, what the Alphabet Tax was, how it came about and how it worked – all from the mouths of those who lived through it, as well as from the pens of those who, for various reasons, made it happen.

Warning: readers may find certain documents or extracts distressing.

We have marshalled the materials discovered in various states of completion at the Central Houses into subject areas, and we've ordered the sections so that the full horror of Coder thought is gradually revealed. These decisions have been made with everyone's best interests at heart. Applications to view the entire archive, including certain materials withheld from public view, will be sensitively processed. Each of the sections made available here begins with a brief note from the archive folk, to give fair warning about whether or to what extent the overall topic that follows is likely to cause distress. Our "PostCode" stories come at the end.

Section one contains a broad selection of Coders' policy documents and manifestos that reveal the theories behind the ATax and the mechanisms used to enforce it. Given the dominant role the buildings played in the Alpha Tax era, we have included two sections of reflections on Central Houses from users of the buildings – on both sides of the fence, as it were. Section two, Standing Witness, contains stories and comments from those of us who had no choice but to visit the Central Houses. Then, in Monumental Systems, we include documents authored by those who played a role in the shaping and delivery of ATax, all of whom chose to support the regime to some extent.

In the Strategic Treatise section we delve deeper into the more toxic waters of ATax. It contains less restricted, more "internal eyes only" accounts of how the Code operated. (We recommend that readers of this section proceed with caution.) Then, in a more hopeful interlude, there follows the Resistance Mechanisms section, which offers some enlightening and heartening accounts from the ATax opposition, the Wall-Es – those who risked everything to work against the horrors of ATax. The Wall-Es were a resistance force, and in opposing the brutalities of the regime they put themselves in great danger.

In Application and Entitlement there are no embellishments. These writings, by a few of the seemingly unguarded, wilfully cruel, hard-line ATax supporters, were written for consumption only by the elite, a tiny readership of believers who often advocated the harshest measures. Many will find this section an uncomfortable read, unbearable even. If it's too hard to stomach, we strongly advise turning the page. This is disturbing stuff, no doubt about it – way beyond the "holding your nose" level of revulsion.

And the page you'll find you've turned to is PostCode Accounts, the penultimate section, comprised of reports and interviews we archivers have gleaned since the Taxers' downfall. It is indicative of how far we've come since those bad old days that these accounts exist at all. Some respondents already look to the future. Some prefer to work on disentangling the threads of what brought us here. As we say in the Endnote, we must do both if we wish to avoid a repetition of the social catastrophe imposed by the ACoders.

1. The AlphaCode Conversion

This collection of strategies, treatises and policies outlines how the Tax was imagined, how it became established, how it was supposed to operate, and how it worked in practice. In documents made available in the archive, it is possible to track the multiple changes to the ACode that were implemented over time, including, most importantly, how the programme was staffed – the watchers and snitchers, the techies too, all of whom played a part in what was done to us. And it was a part; they might as well have been onstage, acting it out. Together they crafted a wicked fairy-tale. Despite what we've discovered, the official line was that the ACode worked so well from the outset there was never any need for alteration; it was perfection itself, blah bloody blah.

However, on reading these documents it becomes clear that due to unforeseen circumstances some of the Code had to be revised, changes that were discreetly implemented by Central Policy. Appropriately enough, language was a significant factor, and some of this is well documented. One major example would be the change of title from Syntax to Code. It's still possible to read about the unforeseen "positive effects", as they saw it, not least the speed with which implementation of the Code became embedded and accepted.

AlphaCode Manifesto #1: Our Steps[9]

This manifesto is produced on behalf of all units labouring under the punitive, blatantly unfair system that marginalises, excludes and ignores them. It is designed to conserve their skills and energy for more relevant activities; in other words, for better things. It provides a more equitable distribution of resources.

1. We declare the AlphaCode Syntax a visionary replacement for the untenable, corrupt and exploitative system of the old order[10]
2. Always right, even when wrong
3. Clear and conspicuous distribution of resources for all
4. Futurity is the now
5. Integration, interconnection and synergy: from concept to delivery
6. Trials and burdens abolished forthwith
7. This is a declaration of goodwill and optimism
8. Fairness is not a concession but the new norm
9. Communication of all levels of implementation at pace is our forever endpoint
10. Doubters will regret their folly
11. AlphaCode is urgent: keep the time
12. New is now, new is us

•

9 This "manifesto", a declaration of purpose suggesting political change, expresses the highly subjective opinions and viewpoint of the person or persons who wrote it. Consequently, "manifesto" has been replaced in AlphaCode's officially approved lexicon with "treatise", a more considered form, a systematic written discourse on a particular subject, something of an essay (more objective).

10 Some on the opposition flank refer to the network as the Alphabet Tax, an abbreviated form of the original: Alphabet Syntax. With this in mind, it has been renominated as the AlphaCode Conversion. The original name endures in some quarters, in part as a rebuttal.

From our files: an example of how the old system of delivery used to work. Open the cover – printed with name, number, date only – and you'll see the pages are divided into squares with perforations, filled with squat capitals on tinted backgrounds that look like an alphabet primer for early learners, like tickets and counterfoils to be filled in and punched and stamped[11] before the exhausted bearer can advance beyond B, or receive 3/6, or pass Go. If they really were tickets, these could structure a lengthy trip. Numbers on the squares may refer to periods of time, or days of the month, or multiple appointments, or number of sentences. On one level it is a system of banking, with deposits or benefits that can be withdrawn only at prescribed times, like legacy assignment payments or pensions. Allowances are bestowed for the number of Hs or Ms in circulation to each unit. <A quarter R provision for you, in week ending L-L/2>, for example. This is an overt acknowledgement of the wider supply-chain issues in concert with individual assessment. To reassure the units, these allowance books (ration books, effectively) were modelled on the pension books used in the early decades of the 20th century.[12]

Here is an approximation of allocations from those early days:
ETAONSHR (1-2 hander) LUOBT (3 hander)
Off with: GJKQUVXYZ / second line: DILNPR

In those days, because of the use of disposable paper and coupons, concerns about material wastage were common. But then, as the book says, "When people lose things,[13] that

---

11 How aggressive were the old ways!

12 This "counter delivery"-style method was useful in the early days; so distant now it seems absolutely ridiculous and wilfully dangerous. Also wasteful of resources in the extreme.

13 This usage of "people" and "things" gives an indication of the shockingly limited understanding of the gravity of the situation.

indicates their lack of need."[14] The letters are time-limited, too: more "only before" than "best before".[15] Deposits can only be used a certain number of times, with a strictly adhered to use-by date, like old-style passwords that timed out, restricting access. Hence, thinking before speaking becomes an essential part of everyday life, requiring much planning on the part of each unit. What do they have to say, and what's the quickest and most efficient way of saying it? With this planning comes much quiet. The deposits are non-transferable; unlike sperm or peas they cannot be frozen for later use. Individual rations are also predicated on national and local averages. Benefits are not lifelong or annual or even seasonal – there is a rolling review structure in place, so benefits are subject to change at any time without warning. From the earliest iterations, sanctions were in place to show that users must take individual responsibility for their beneficial treatment. There are always criminal factions who seek to override processes and codes, even to break laws. Some say they too deserve our care and attention rather than punishment, for they are unable to control their anti-social impulses and therefore must be ill and in need of help. [For those with Level VI access, see: The Kindest Cut: Ultimate Sanction Options Offer a Robust Response.]

Because units perceive their appointments at Central House/s to be for them only – as in no other units visible in the building, no interaction at entry and exit points (which only rarely now have to be cleared by the greeters) – they also perceive that any activation of the red feather is directed at them only. This tells them: your letters are finished for this period of treatment. In many instances, the

14 Research into single-dose brain chemistry alterants, which would obviate the need for such delivery mechanisms, is ongoing. Also considered but now deemed extravagant and unnecessary: brainwave interceptors, chemo transfer and iridology implants through walk-past screen images. For now, the red feather system continues to function adequately; see above.

15 Or use 'em, lose 'em, as we sometimes say – off duty, mind.

red feather is allotted to a Central House/s for a portion of a day, a whole day, or even a week, to catch the eye of all unit attendees, leading to a substantial fall in letter outgoings and a rise in the quiet of wellbeing.

Long gone are the days when watchers actually carried a supply of red feathers to distribute to any whingers and whiners they'd caught over-indulging (or not) in their letters. Ultimately this was wasteful of resources – collecting, preserving, printing, painting or dyeing, and distribution – as the concerns about mass printing and paper waste were in the early-form voucher books and passes. Not least, the term "pass" was a mistake – obvious enough now! – as it gave the impression of something being achieved, something gained and endorsed, leading to a completely misplaced and inappropriate sense of complacency.

The allotted portion of benefit was paid in exchange for delivering the page or ticket to be torn out, annotated and verified in some way. As a form of control and containment, this worked fairly well in both the short- and long-term.[16] Trialling this as a method of delivery was suggested in planning discussions. It had its adherents but was ultimately discarded, with the aforementioned concerns about resources, which in the early days were precious and expensive, and later became unavailable.

We have been tasked with improving the allocation indicator context through the development and application of AlphaCode Conversion. It is an honour to be entrusted with this weighty, far-reaching programme, and needless to say we do not take our responsibilities lightly.

•

16 See earlier, on disposability concerns: in concert with the persuasive "fear implant" factor (see below).

Treatise
Cost Benefit Analysis: Restructuring and Recycling

Our system responds to wastefulness as a priority because this state of affairs cannot be allowed to continue. Why should more resources be given to those who can't use what they already have? Or simply don't use, whether through ineptitude, laziness, or sheer pigheadedness.[17] It's not fair to them and not good for the rest of us. Why should we continue to prop up those who already cost more and take up valuable space with their blithering nonsense, their pestilential opinions? Too many words; not enough space for the rest of us. We have to ask what good it does them. We have to consider the cost, the detrimental long-term implications and effects on the rest of us. Even whether there *are* any pluses. What is the nature of benefit if those who supply it are having to support those who receive it twice over, in delivery and then again in mopping up their fails? How long must this situation be allowed to continue before we address the problem?

Once we'd recognised the opportunity we had during the early, quiet times of shutdown, we considered the messages our overly relaxed approach was communicating and were faced with a clear response to many of the above questions. It was time to look again at the system and give it a thorough overhaul. We had to be sure that in the post-Hardship era we would not be accused of creating a culture that fosters habituation or inertia. We did not want to be responsible for a system that takes when it ought to give. Remember the old saying, "Less is more"? How wrong that is! We believe without a shadow of a doubt that more (benefit) is less (burden) and more (ease) for all of us. We want to help. To repurpose another old phrase: "That's what we're here

17 Regrettably, research tells us that "all of the above" is an accurate assessment of the situation.

for." We want to provide something extra for those experiencing difficulty. If our help, which we all pay for, has undesirable consequences, then we must do our utmost to guard against them.[18] It may take some time to ascertain how best to do this. A degree of trial and error may be involved.

The phrase "lessons learned" is no longer used; our work has obviated the need for it. But lessons have indeed been learned, finally, indisputably. Such as: the units should not be expected to comprehend the methods of provision; they need only be compliant. (Being grateful would be nice, too, but that's an unlikely prospect entailing, as it does, greater understanding than they can be credited with.) Also, explaining how the methods of provision worked might give rebels and naysayers the impression that other options were available, allowing them to suggest that other options were preferable and the methods of provision were therefore up for debate. This, I stress, is totally undesirable! In terms of social mores, hierarchies, and the new class structure, our programme is self-regulating.[19]

Although our approach is one of universality, some minor issues have arisen. We realised that due to The Hardship it was our duty to extend what was once known as parental care to much of the population. Initially it was assumed that the provision of care would be uniform across the entire age range. Indeed, it was a given that doing otherwise would be discriminatory, in an unconscionably retrograde way. But we can never rest comfortably under such assumptions, and world-class ministry members are developing solutions designed to root them out.

With this in mind as one of our defining principles, when

18 To be clear, we must try to safeguard against any *desirable* unforeseen consequences.
19 Unspoken, we might say!

the question of lifelong parity was revisited we realised this concept needed much more work. AlphaCode is about caring at all levels. Our duty of care is not just to the young and old. Often it is the generations in the middle that are most in need of assistance and education. Parity of benefit across age, unchanging provision at any stage of life is, in fact, deeply unfair. It falsely assumes that needs and requirements remain unchanged throughout whole lifespans.

Without wishing to generalise about age-related behaviours, those middle generations may ideally be placed to reap the greatest reward from the renewed programme. They are fully aware of the extra weight they carry needlessly and of the immediate relief the programme will deliver. There may, of course, be difficulties with the old, who often as not have grown used to floundering about in their customary ways. Even before The Hardship, the old were known to be stubbornly resistant to change, though generally given to compliance in the long term. The young may not suffer from such drawbacks, but they may lack the necessary behavioural qualities or indeed the necessary degree of concentration.

•

Staffing

Once into the Big Quiet, compliance with Code benefit levels and behaviours was overseen and administered by a newly established special force: AlphaWatch. Due to cuts, staff shortages and massively overgenerous sick leave[20] – the watch patrols had to step back from their first base of engagement. Their 24/7 patrols, which involved listening, watching, following, checking, on the streets, in shops, pubs

20 Even something referred to as "holiday" provision.

and other meeting places, gave us some big wins in the early years. They could and did intervene at any time. Armed and uniformed, they were an imposing presence. When a patrol stopped a group of units and told them to stop talking – about the Quiet, about The Hardship, about anything at all – it worked, they were immediately silenced. Then the Code announced that some words were banned, quite randomly at first – war, attack, rights. We toyed with banning letters at this time too, Q Z I for starters, but decided it was too soon. Not for long, though – all systems go!

From that point on, it wasn't long before the system was set up so that units received a monthly stipend and carried identity cards that also indicated their level of benefit, and the watchers checked the cards on a frequent stop-and-search basis. Living quarters and gardens were also covered. At any time, in any place, units grew to expect to have to show their cards to the watchers, explain what the noise – effectively extra non-ratified expenditure – was about <Too Many Words, what's going on?>, and take any necessary follow-up measures. No regularity, no privacy, no escape.

The huge numbers of watchers initially taken on, essential at the time to establish the Code, could not be maintained indefinitely. To address this, a large force of plain-clothes influencers was signed up. They were flattered into thinking they were doing the right thing, serving the community. If someone was cheating the system, they should be reported, right? And the more of those wishy-washy, lily-livered, smug, goody-goody, equality-nonsense liberal types who could have the watchers informed of their behaviour, the better. Sad that so many of the influencers turned out to have family and friends who were that way inclined, but you can't do them favours just because they're your people, now can you?

The influencers were reliable to a fault and effective to the nth degree. The watchers got much valuable information from them and from their own patrols that was necessary for enforcement. The influencers, deeply embedded in the community, reported back to the watchers, letting them know who was taking liberties by spouting dangerous talk – whatever the topic, it was just too much! Even at this stage the system was so productive that the Code became normalised and self-perpetuating, helped enormously by the fear instilled in the populace by the influencer/snitchers and watchers. The investment in the AlphaWatch force, initially considered eye-wateringly expensive due to its massive size, proved extremely valuable and paid impressive dividends.

As the success of each extension of the Code became more obvious, reducing the deployment of watchers became possible. Not that they'd worked themselves out of a job – quite the contrary; they'd demonstrated precisely how important the work was. The reduction in cost through repositioning the watchers was another huge win – taking them off the streets, in many cases, and situating them behind screens. Some were encouraged to retrain as trustees, others took advantage of an enormously generous retirement package.[21]

The watchers' other role, an even more fundamental one, was to listen. Or at least to give the impression that they were able to hear everything. How it worked, or seemed to work, was that watchers entered every living space to fit these gizmos – "extensions to utilities" was what we said they were – to oversee and overhear every move, every word, every letter. As if anyone, even the operatives, were going to sit and listen to all that drivel, even if we ever got round to actually paying them for doing so.

21 Money was involved, as was relocation and a change of identity due to the fear of reprisals.

Then, shortly after the watchers had installed the pretend recorders – out of reach of the units and with Danger! Shock Alert! Hazard! signs taped up everywhere – the techies arrived to activate them. Techies schmeckies! "Specialist knowledge?" – do me a favour. Looking back, that was one of the most difficult things to organise: finding enough people to do the necessary acting. The Watchers and the techies had to be different people, no cross-over, to limit in number those who knew the surveillance wasn't real, that the recorders didn't work in any way other than as a reminder not to talk. The techies paid the price, of course. Couldn't risk them blabbing, whereas the watchers were safe because they didn't know the recorders were fake. They were just setting the scene, as it were. As in, "This system is so complex it takes several visits by different experts to install it." The techies died for their fellows, for their country. In the line of duty, for sure.

The units may not have been convinced in the beginning but, for what started as a bit of a caper for the Coders, it had legs. Most of the units were scared enough to have doubts – maybe the gizmo did work, maybe we should do what we're told, they know best, they're doing what they can. They hear us. Outdoors CCTV was everywhere already, so they were seen to be fitting extensions to that too. CCTV now had sound as well as vision! That was the story. That's how we reeled them in.

It had to look as though every unit's portion of letters was minutely calibrated using an impenetrably complex scientific method. It wasn't. We never realised how well it would work without having to do anything of the sort. Not an oven-ready system at all, more like already digested. Such a shame; if we'd known it would be so easy, we could have finished our work much earlier.

•

When the initial rollout design, the much-trumpeted metrics and metadata and its precisions were found to be burdensome and unnecessary, alternatives had to be found and swiftly implemented, and the changeover had to be not only smooth but unremarked. The use of metadata relied on appliances and habits that were archaic and no longer applicable to the vast majority of the Gifted. There were, albeit briefly, concerns about "data protection" and "client privacy".[22] Once the terminology changed and there was no longer any unitary expectation of privacy, such concerns became a cause of worry only when mentioned, which was almost never.

Metadata could tell us if an act of communication had taken place: that was all we needed to know. It was crucial in determining the level of benefit appropriate for each unit. It could provide necessary information about the where, the who and the when, but as to the what, the content and detail of the communication, it provided no insight. Since there was no content as such, metadata was of greater use. The smartphone and the internet, still platforms for communication in the early stages of the Conversion, did not provide enough data for calculations to be made at the necessary level of intricacy. Even with the so-called "creative accounting" of deep-data wizards, who'd had departments created specially for them, this was still not enough. Eventually we had to turn to other methods. Things change and the world and its technologies move on.

It was some time into the second shutdown[23] before the amnesty for phonesets reached its deadline and signals

22 Bear in mind, this was some time ago.
23 Or the third, can't quite recall now.

were jammed on most networks. That was long after "social media" had been identified as a significant threat.[24] The internet, once it had been made inaccessible, imploded. None of the other devices could survive the removal of internet access; dial-up dealers were shamed as pirates and metaphorically "hung from the yardarm". There were those among us who believed passionately in the rewards of the "140-characters" approach. This number of characters was patently far too extensive, but as a method for limiting unwarranted interactions it had proven worth.

Equally, the networks that defined themselves as of a "work"-related nature (another legacy term, I know) could not survive in the new society in which we found ourselves. There was no longer any place for such networks, living as we are in the now, among our own people, in small, discrete communities. They were without goal or intent and lacked any repositioning potential. And what need was there for assignments, as this "work" activity was re-termed? Health and learning services were there for those who needed them, and, along with funds provided for training and equipment, compulsory loans were made, a benefit to be permanently repaid through contributions [see also: Repayments: the price of deferral].

Centralised food agencies (known as "banks") were established, responding to the complex needs of the many, those lacking the capacity to enjoy and fully utilise their raft of benefits. In time, with the help of retraining programmes, many units were found to be much "more able" in these respects than had previously been thought possible. Now that this is understood and incorporated into the system, the devastating effects of the underestimation of unit poten-

24 "Social media" remained burdensome for those of us who retained access in order to monitor it, the few hardy souls who continued to check what was once known as "popular taste and opinion".

tial have been mitigated substantially. The effect of cascading information down the relevant strategic staircase was that potential became incorporated into assessment.[25]

Many methods were trialled with unparalleled speed and efficiency. Quietly, to avoid causing concern, we went through standardisation,[26] a closed accounting system,[27] and randomised short-term allocation. The last method was particularly well received by our superiors. When we settled on the highly systemic Tracey method, it was still so new that some were mystified by it and (ahem) blind to its potential. Building on earlier systems of looking and listening, Tracey provides a source of immeasurable clarity about who has what. We increased the potential of this tried-and-tested profiling method that had, for unfathomable reasons, been discontinued.[28] We brought it into the new era by extending its rather limited ambit that focused on race only, adding the t as a reminder of the primary importance of "testing", "tracking" and "tracing". Tracey profiling's simplicity is what makes it such a resounding success.

After suitable training, the trustee makes a professional assessment of the unit by looking (covering race and gender; sometimes also religion, sexuality, belief) or by listening (covering class, area, accent, education). When carried out professionally, this process is swift, accurate and highly effective.

First: observation – what is immediately apparent in face-

25 "Potential" and its measurement are the subject of *Fulfilling Potential: the Alpha Road,* available at Central House/s and mandatory reading during staff induction.

26 One size fits all – with emphasis placed on the universality of the system – was a personal favourite for its consummate simplicity and fairness.

27 This was discontinued, removed from consideration, as it was evidenced to be too open to fraud.

28 High on the long list of "dubious politics past".

to-face assessment or "looking".[29]

Second: what is quickly ascertainable once the unit is in "speaking" mode.

The sheer simplicity of assessment using Tracey was, for some, a cause for suspicion. As though nothing useful and worthwhile could be anything other than hideously complex and time-consuming!

Instead of extracting data to analyse and count, Tracey works by looking. That's it. That's really all there is to it. And a little bit of listening, too, when the units talk, if they really must. A small acknowledgement of time is given. A little leeway, just to be on the safe side. All trustees are capable of carrying out the assessment.[30] You see, you hear, you decide: it's done. No additional process is needed to complete the assessment. It's efficacy is indisputable. The job of greeter and signposter also relies on Tracey. The greeter/signposter is the first port of call, the first line of resistance, i.e. between staff and units. It's about protection, in order to monitor behaviour and avoid the possibility of advantage being taken of any of the waiting areas.[31]

In all these ways, AlphaCode is a self-limiting system that will, in the not-too-distant future, make itself redundant as more of the Gifted enter full recovery. At which point, the investment following The Hardship – the time and toil – will pay huge dividends. The ACode is designed to add greater advantage to

29 "Face-to-face" is slightly misleading. Protective screens, masks or reflectors are in place for reasons of safety and hygiene (see below).

30 The idea that trustees are a credited, accomplished part of the system is not incorrect, but perhaps the level of trustee input has been given something of a shine here, considering that their skills are only minimally above those of the Gifted (indeed, switches between these levels are not unknown).

31 Some waiting areas still exist, for use if delays have impacted refurbishments; see Central House/s updates to check.

those already enjoying receipt. Furthermore, it simplifies social so-called "services". Fewer responses are possible, and those that are are shorter and simpler.[32] "Yes" or "no" are the only options, but "yes" is the right one! Think of the savings! It's about improvement and ease and simplification and advantages for all. It's money, that's it.

•

HMRC#012 Draft **5 – with editor's comments

"It has become apparent that ..."
>No, this needs to be more active, displaying more warmth, vitality ...

"There can be no more worthwhile aspiration than ..."
>Nnnah ...

"What more worthwhile goal can there be than delivering our fellows from ..."
>Noooo – what if someone made a list of other goals that might prove more worthwhile? And what if someone could show that we're doing something different from what we said the Code allows? I can't quite believe I'm putting this down on paper.

"While we deplore any kind of fuss – the rewards of hard work are recognition enough – it is impossible to overstate/ it cannot be over-emphasised how ..."

"This is groundbreaking in concept and its delivery has brought change long awaited ~~and, to be fair, long thought elusive~~ in implementation. It will be transformative for our society. A major contribution to wellbeing for the modern age, going forward."

32 Sometimes referred to (quietly) in the office as the "x-grunt".

"An unprecedented breadth of application across the sections of society most in need. Lives will be changed beyond recognition, ~~forever,~~ for the betterment of all."

Be less specific – less possibility for comeback.

"It is generous in outline and in substance. It is a ~~root and branch~~ systemic (and hearts and minds) reform, more than reform, all-encompassing, a major departure, ~~[revolutionary, radical]~~ dynamic, extreme from the entrenched, partial, complicated, ~~tired~~ archaic and, it must be said, ineffective, systems that we~~, to be frank,~~ have struggled to operate with any real effect ~~for some time now~~."

Too wordy. Needs to feel/sound more immediate.

"Open up a new world specially designed to alleviate the burden for those already benefitting from the improved/lightened requirements. ~~Why should those who might already be struggling have to manage with this too?~~"

Nah, not quite the right tone.

"This is a customised creative solution fitting for the new century."

Boom boom! That's more like it!

•

Manifesto Agreement for the Gifted –
to be signed by all ~~recips~~[33]

We embrace the programme
We attend all sessions because they're for the best
We comply
We work together
We all want the same thing
Signature _____[34]

33 No longer in use; substitute "units".
34 By which we mean an x, nothing more.

Our vision of the future wins. It distils down to two short sentences: AlphaCode for all. Alpha Benefit Cures and Cares.

•

More Scripted Phrases for Use in Encounters
with the Gifted

Repetition is reinforcement
Doing the right thing is our mantra
Benefit is our business and this is how we all benefit
We are always agreeable and in agreement
Choose benefit
Surrendering is winning
We defer to us
Mandatory co-operation is the way forward
Just say yes
Together we can do this
New ways for new times
Open your arms to surrender
Observance is for now
We're all in this together

•

*HMRC#047 Draft **8, n.d. Annual Agenda*

1. allowances
2. Gifted access
3. open-door policies for allocation
4. timekeeping
5. comprehensive coverage
6. tunnel and lift safety [see also: "Erstwhile Spaces"]
7. red feather designs
8. recovery procedures

9. breaks
10. NDAs
11. staff development
12. gross misconduct
13. ~~trans-Central social~~ [cancelled due to safety concerns]
14. coverage levels and extra benefit rollout
15. thought-shower curtains
16. best practice solutioning
17. buy-in and enforcement
18. clients and herding cats
19. quick wins: retreading the strategic staircase
20. telling the story
21. creative compliance
22. seamless adoption
23. client-centricity – the new mantra
24. road maps for the future
25. no "I" in team – no "me" in Central
26. aob: penalties for unauthorised usage. Basic set. Political football. Elite problem

•

DM from Conference Keynote Speaker –
received by conference attendee.[35]
security level clearance *****

"Why? You're still asking why? Because why should others pay? Because we are right. In all fairness, it's the way forward. Why? Really!? To shut them up, of course. It's not like they have anything worth saying. We can silence them. We can. We can shut them up.

"Why should they maintain this absurd belief in what was

35 The attendee who received the DM and passed it on described themself (gender unknown) as an ex-Code strategist; still unverified at time of publication.

called 'free speech'? What's free about it? Nothing is without cost, and cost is the measure of worth. To suggest that speech costs nothing is an insult to the ears. It's nothing less than wholesale, systematic theft, stealing from us all and costing plenty. Some were never in any doubt that 'free speech' applied to them. It's about levelling up. But did they accept and adjust? No! Others persisted with the fallacy that they were better, they had it owing to them, and on that basis felt they had to say something, anything.

"It's a ridiculous idea that they can say whatever they like whenever they like. Always was. Nothing has changed on that score. Their mindless drivel takes up too much time, and it costs us too – not least being bored rigid by their nonsense. No, I don't want to know, and I don't see why I have to hear it (speaking generally, as well as for myself). They'll just witter on forever in their personal echo chambers if we let them, if the gloomsters and doomsters have their way. We have more pressing matters to deal with in our world. What the nay-sayers say, and what I say, is 'Just don't say it!'

"C'mon, between you and me, let's cut the crap. We're off the record now. We know we can shut them up, and we should. We owe it to society. Not the Big Quiet, we can do better than that – we could have Neverending Quiet. Imagine the peace! There'll be no complaints. How delightfully quiet the streets will be! Post-Hardship shutdown as the new normal, the perfect grounding for full AlphaCode implementation. There won't be any backlash because everyone will be happy with what they've got. And soon they will – well, might – think before they speak, and if they don't it'll cost them dear. That's another manifesto promise! Imagine the pleasures of a quiet life.

"AlphaCode Conversion we call it – it's all there in the

name. We converted nothing into something, with some messaging here, a degree of re-enforcement there, and a lot of play-acting. We had to put in a hell of a lot of hours, and the watchers, whistlers and snitchers, as well as actors posing as tech installers, had to be paid for. But we paid peanuts and we got a good job done, fit for purpose.

"We did what we had to do: find a way to tax their words. All done through the new benefit system. AlphaCode: the answer to all our troubles! No further discussion is needed, as I said in the speech. That's the generosity of it: taking time to ascertain how to make it work for everybody. Taxes are for the common good, after all, a way for everyone to make a contribution to society. Progressive taxes, that's the thing. Progressive, as in the more you need the more you get and the more help you're entitled to. It'll also shut the units up. That's the best part of it."

2. Standing Witness

When the AlphaCode was still fresh in memory, we began asking people to talk to us for the archive – interviews about their histories. We said, "Tell us whatever you want about it." Later we asked them to talk on particular themes – family, Wall-Es, the future, and their experience of the Code's various processes. Time and again, Central Houses came up. Because so many people talked about them, we decided to start with a section on the buildings themselves. Central Houses made it happen, made it all possible.

Even more than the watchers and their squealer sidekicks, the hearers and the techies, the quiets and the benefits themselves, Central Houses were so ... well ... so central to their plan, to what everyone suffered. That's how it worked. The buildings were supposed to be where all the info and data that watchers brought in was put, together with the non-existent recordings from our living spaces, for the trustees to make their fine-tuned assessments. As if. Some of us thought even then that none of it made sense, and we were right all along. If they were senior enough, the Taxers must have known that the Code system was based on nothing. Getting us to believe in a joined-up nothing was the system.

Central Houses were specifically designed as enforcement zones, and an extraordinary amount of detail went into making each and every one of them as hostile an environment as possible. Who knew – and I'm borrowing here from the account of one of the contributors to this section – that architecture could be made to be so malign? It starts with shelter and look where it can go. As you'll read in these pages, they really couldn't have designed Central House better. The interviews are folded into a single conversation, though the conversations were many, all involving people who were under the thumb of the ACode and whose daily lives were ruled over by the imposing bulk of Central House. As mentioned in our introduction, recording these conversations for the archive is an essential way of rescuing ourselves from the fear we feel to this day.

So here are the testimonies from those at the sharp end, sharing their experiences of how ATax was administered and brought to bear on them at the Central Houses.

•

They call it the AlphaCode, housed in Central House, where benefit is imposed. We call it the Alphabet Tax. Well, they started it with their AlphaSyntax rubbish. Whatever, it's delivered in the ABCastle, and it's AlphaBetCastle in full, for those that can. Or we call it the ABC. We're the Delites, short for Deliterati and shorter is always better now. They call us Gifted because they want us to believe they're giving us presents. Gifted we may be, but we're not stupid. It's all about us, though. That's something we can agree on. Maybe the only thing.

> The future starts here. The sign says so, or it used to. You can still read it but it's like reading the inscription on a tomb. A massive one, not just for a single person. Maybe for everybody, for us all. It's writ large, very large, chiselled on a stone slab, and it sits above an archway leading into the hallway. Whoever designed this, they wanted to create an impression, get a loud message out. "Get this, everybody, every one of you who walks through this entrance, through this hallway. You should know that the future is this: Central House/s are the place of delivery of the AlphaCode." So you come through the front door, into a lobby area transparent enough to make it unthreatening, to dispel any misgivings about the step you're taking,

about what you're getting yourself into. Welcoming, almost. It makes passing from exterior to interior, an outsider becoming an insider, seem almost negligible. And that's your first mistake. Not that choice was involved. Once you're safely in, your future is written, it's done.

No one believed it. Who would have thought that architecture had such power? I mean, they're just buildings, right? But coercion isn't in it. It isn't only that it enforces particular modes of behaviour and excludes – denies the possibility of – any other forms. It's that it allows no authority other than its own. You do what it tells you, you can't help yourself. I guarantee that building users are terrorised and pressurised into doing its bidding, with threats of untold damage as drivers of compliance. If an inanimate object could be charged in court, in the old courts of law, this building, this Central House place, might be found guilty of aggressive manipulation. The system is kittenish by comparision. Compliance is enforced by design at every level.

The cladding looks like it's from a computer game but less realistic. This is rock-bottom design: poor, unimaginative, uninspired. The shops at the base are still standing but long since closed. A squatter zone that even squatters won't use, it's that bad. Forbidding. A dusty plaque says this was once a government building: Public Guardianship/Court of Protection (guardian? protection? – that can't be right).

Heard this one used to be thought a special place. Someone said so. Before The Hardship, that is. Quite a place, apparently. Hard to see, now. When the buildings on the next block were cleared away

– just gone one morning, no idea how or why – you were able to get a better look at it. But really, why would you want to? So then it was like an island, the traffic going round it, clockwise. Not exactly a roundabout. Stranded in all its glory, sore thumb or what?

It's true, there was stone, and you didn't see much of that anymore. That's what it was built from, not just extruded shite. Maybe if it was cleaned up it might make a difference. Whatever it was for, the entire interior has been stripped out to erase any reminders. They don't want us to remember, they don't like that. That's backwards-looking. Like another memorial.

Everything happens at Central House. That's where you have to go. For a consultation, they call it. About what's best for you. To suit your needs and make sure we're all levelled up the same. They called it a fulfilment centre – for everything you need and want. We still called it ABCastle, at the beginning anyway. They said it was where the real issues facing big society would be tackled. Bread and butter, all in it together, so we had to come to the same place. That's what they said. They were very strict about it: we had to come there as many times as they said, and the more often we came the better the treatment we received. That meant our benefit was higher. "You're getting the maximum facetime" – that's how they put it.

You have to go so they know you've been. Some-one knows you've been there, you keep getting benefit. They can only tell you what you're getting this time around. The next time it might be com-pletely different. The personal touch, the one-on-

one, they call it. That's how they're helping everyone and Central House is the safe place for us to
have the conversation. Other than that, we have to
count it all up, every D and C, not go over the limit.
I'm only telling it like they tell us. It's for confiden-
tiality. That's what we get there, the confidence
that our needs are being assessed and addressed in
the proper place and in the correct manner. Eras-
ing inequality is a serious business and sited with
that in mind. Central House is where they have the
case notes and specialists on hand if anything goes
wrong. If we don't go for the appointments, who's
to say we're not doing wrong, taking advantage.
Only ourselves to blame if we go over our benefit,
but everyone feels the pain. We have to take it on
– we just can't afford it anymore. Enough of all the
opinions and bitching, we all have to keep quiet. Let
those who know take the lead. It's the only way.
They need to know where we are, that we're
within reach at all times, so that if our condition
worsens, needs urgent attention, they're there to
help as soon as possible.

It's because we're part of the system, same system
for everyone, keeps us together, on track. When
you get inside the consulting room, it can be just a
signature that's wanted, then you're off again.
Sometimes they tell you when the next one is.
Other days they'll ask questions about your
progress, how you're feeling, about your Ps and Ts,
how you're eating, your Bs and Gs, how it's going,
all that. It's the Castle of our Is and Yous, can say
that there. They put a mark to say you've come.
They say: "We'll increase your benefit this time –
you're going up to a two-hander, no more Cs and
Ms to deal with. Well done, you!"

You've never been in any place like it. Street-facing, looks abandoned. Closed up, closed down – take your pick. Enter at your peril. Can't see through the windows. You wouldn't want to go in there – not even going to be warm. From the humiliating scale of the point of entry onwards, efforts are made to ensure belittlement, so visitors are cowed, unsteady. Entry procedures and protocols sharpen the point. The urgency to find the right place, in order to avoid the further benefits that will ensue, is exacerbated by a lack of signage and consequent uncertainty of how that can be achieved. Lighting furthers this effect, "deluminating" rather than its opposite. Can't see your way clear to anywhere. Paths take unexpected angles. Unusual inclines that, followed by steps in an opposite direction, seem to serve no purpose. That's because they don't. Or sometimes it's a purpose you really don't want to know about.

You think it's special, a one-off. At the beginning anyway. But it's only because it's the first official building like that that anyone has been inside. It's more like a spooky funhouse at the fair, but not really that, much more sinister. After a while, not long, really (not long enough!), you almost get used to it, because all the Centrals are like that – anywhere that's about the Coders, like official. Same Central name but in different places. But you don't get accustomed to it, that's the whole point. It's not about becoming comfortable in finding your way around and knowing where you're going or anything like that. They want you on edge, always uncertain. That's what you have to get used to. That's how it's designed to be. What's around the next corner and are you sure you're on the right floor? And what will happen if you're not in the right area. What you recognise soon enough is that kind of feeling – twitchy, guilty, uncomfortable.

You experience fear when you're anywhere near it, because you just don't know, you never quite know what's going on, what's there. But you don't really ever get used to the feeling either, because you don't get any closer to knowing. That's a success story for them. They've got you exactly where they want you. And although knowing that makes you furious, you know there's nothing you can do about it except get furiouser and furiouser.

Maybe the first couple of times you go, there's a sense of mystery. You're worried about it because you don't know what's coming. After that, you already know it's frightening. Move along (slowly, mind), nothing to see here. Not for you, anyway. Surely the place wasn't built for this. Is that even possible? It's bad enough that the Taxers are doing what they're doing and that they've got these places to do it in. But making this building for that purpose … what kind of sick animal would do that? And not only a feeling, there's a look, too. Or maybe it's the lack of those things: the lack of clarity, the feeling of strangeness and disruption that often comes when a place has been repurposed for other uses.

The illegibility is deliberate, internally and externally. On the exterior, there are no signs to indicate the building's purpose or who's allowed to enter. It's just blank, unresponsive, unadorned, dull. There's no signposting on any façade, and in the interior the labels or indicators to advise on location or route or – oh please! – show you the way are barely there, hardly readable. Orientation made fearful, free from markers or views. And Central House can be hard enough to find in the first place, even though they're huge buildings and, you would have thought, unmissable. They really make it easy to miss your time.

It's a funny feeling, like being blocked off. No, blocked in. You can't see into the next room or up the corridor. Can't see your way to anywhere. No long view, not much light either. If they do let you pass, it's only as far as another short stop, another check-in, yet another room with nothing in it, nothing to see there. Nothing on the walls but white, but not ever fresh and new. Fashioned to look always in need of a wash and brush-up. It's well rundown. Pretty soon you give in – well, I did. You stop trying to work out where you are and how it all fits together. You do what they say, you go where and when they say to go. Stop when they say stop. It's much simpler and less hassle. Less frightening too, in a way.

You're told not to move off the route, but it doesn't keep to a single path. Circulation is a minefield. Long passages you can't see the end of, corners you can't see round to know what's coming. Long waits enforced. Faceless. Announcements from a speaker one visit, others it's pindrop quiet and the real-person voice and the recorded one say contradictory things. Numbers and tickets that don't match up. So you're always getting it wrong. Arbitrary security ejections can happen any time, without warning. Large doors belittle you. Chairs, if there are any, are fixed to the floor. Child-sized they are too, brightly coloured, furnishing a building that kids will never enter (please god). Stairs only on this side of the building. Someone said there are lifts on the

other. Who for? Steep and narrow and dark, or so
bright you feel sick. Sicker.

You walk down a corridor. You don't know what to
expect. It might happen almost immediately; or
other days you walk for what seems like miles, then
nearly get stuck in a blind corner in almost complete darkness. You weren't expecting that. Of
course you weren't! There are these small open-
ings to rooms that are difficult to negotiate, sometimes with stepped-up thresholds that make it even
harder to enter. It all adds to the effect. Most of the
corridors are like neverending roads but where
you can't see into the distance. By the time you get
to where you're supposed to be, you're always
worried in case you've missed the slot. It's often
dark, too, so finding your way to the right place
isn't easy. According to the welcome delegate
you're always late even when in fact you're early.
Then there's the times when you know you're not
late but it's no odds what you think, to them you're
somehow not on time so they've still got you. It's
increased benefit time. Always for our own good,
obvs.

You're already locked into the system, strapped
down into it. And you can get locked in the building too. That's what I heard. Special treatment
when you get close to full recovery. Never happened to me, thankfully. Trapdoors in rooms that
look like cupboards are rumoured to lead to secret
spaces. Staircases that go nowhere. Fireplaces that
take you into other rooms. Were people stuck in
there for good, incarcerated in that place? Where
did they all go, those in care? Taken away somewhere far beyond and never seen again, so changed

are they? They could never come back to pick up their former (so-called) lives, nor would they be recognisable in them. The absolutely Gifted, I'm talking about. And they're not going to be able to tell the story themselves, now are they?

The way in, when you first came to that Central House, used to be through the side hall. Remember that? A long walk up to the desk, and there's a couple of greeters sitting there. Like watchers, only inside. Don't ask you anything, don't want to see anything, check your chip, scan you, like they used to back then. These days, nothing; if they even notice you walk past, that's a lot. And you're in. That was before, though. Now you walk round to the other door, and there's never anyone there to answer the bell – if it rings, even. But it opens right away. You wonder whether it's open for anyone to walk in that way. And there's heat. For a couple of minutes you're happy, almost: there's this, at least. Old habits! Even when the system tells you to check in, or jog on, you know you've had that. Inside, a warm minute or two. Inside, and no rain, no traffic, no watchers you can see.

The size of the arch you have to walk under, the heft of the stone, makes you feel small and vulnerable. Lets you know you're totally insignificant. You really get that, loud and clear. Whatever this place was used for then isn't obvious. These days it marks where any and all prospects end, where any dreams you may have managed to cling to are over. Like a portal to the future, or a gravestone. Go through: the hereafter awaits you. So when they decided the arch had to come down, a few of us were press-ganged into being gophers and carriers.

It wasn't that the Syntax, as they called it then, wasn't about the coming transformation – it certainly was. But maybe one of them thought it wasn't establishing quite the right tone. False expectations were being created – maybe that was the fear. Future ends here, more like. And maybe they wanted to slightly minimise the possibility of the block falling off and crushing those below – although if it was us Delites, well, we'd be said to have died in the service of others, so that's all right.

They needn't have worried (I'm guessing they didn't) because the "future" turned out to be made of almost nothing, billions of tiny bubbles of plastic, of no weight whatsoever. Say what you want, they're not slow on the uptake – quick as you can, as we were dismantling it, the future! – we were told there was to be no pictures or serious consequences would follow. But maybe they're not so clued in after all: as if anyone had a camera, even then! Good job they don't realise that. Makes them a tad uncertain, fearful of a power we don't have anymore.

The arch day, that was the first time any of us had been in there. With its closed plan designed to look accidental, qualities of shelter or comfort or fitness for use are irrelevant. It's a building already in lockdown, whose users are condemned in perpetuity to obstructed circulation, never being able to see through to the next space to see what's coming, or who. But you never share a space, never see others like us – just the faint echo of footfalls that aren't yours and someone else's grubby fingerprints on the handrails. Hopeful, anyhow. It's not just you in there. You're not alone. Whether you're down the corridor or in your next assessment, this is a purpose-built deadspace, full of stale air and corners where no light can reach. It is ill-at-ease in physical form, done so well, so thoroughly, that we feel it for as many visits as we have to make. The empty windows and bricked-up doors of Central House make it a masterpiece of discomfort, for maximum displacement. It's a design for dis-ease, with no hope of respite. The way it is, there's no knowing where other people get sent. They have to follow other tracks.

Someone who used to do that work tells me about it. He says he shouldn't be telling me. Doesn't say why the work stopped. And I don't know why he's telling me. At the time I think it must be some kind of trap. So I listen, don't speak, no reaction they can get me on. It's still hard to understand, but he says the buildings are made to be like that because they want people to feel unsure, unwelcome, always in the wrong place. He says the ways you get around to where you're going are meant to be confusing – if you get lost and miss your time, that's less work for them, right? You've failed and you're deleted, bish bosh, he says. I tell him how you have to remember this long route, up and down and round about. No signs or nothing.

And the lights – they've really got a problem with that. They should get someone in to sort it out. Most of the time the lights aren't working at all. And because there's no windows, there's no light coming in from outdoors to help. Sometimes a bit of corridor is bright white or there's a light from below, almost at floor level. Very spooky. He tells me that's how they want it, it's not that the lights aren't working. When I first hear this, I wonder if he's all right. Or if things have got to him. Pinch of salt and all that; what to believe and what you want to believe.

He says "Just you wait. When they start sending you all over – one week far over east, then out across the river, then back here for a week – that's when you realise what it's about. More confusing. More room to fail, see? The other Centrals are all different, but they're all done up like that, so wherever you go you still have the same feeling, only more so, because of the lack of familiarity." That's what he says. Crazy, I think. Until I know better. People are kept separate, it's written into the system in case anyone talks, gets ideas. Because who's to stop you using more? Who's going to know? You ever thought of that? Do I look stupid? He thinks I'm going to fall for that? Really? Never saw him again, anyway.

But then I think about it. This isn't Big Brother or anything. Those watchers aren't around anymore, it's only the spies and how many can there really be? They can't keep track of everything you say. I walked off, then, scared. That's the big question, really. Bigger even than asking why they'd want to do this in the first place. And why did we let it happen? How did they get away with it? You don't get used to it. I don't want to. But at the same time I want to hang on to what I've got. Maybe I'm too scared to risk losing more. Whatever he says, I want to try to hang on.

On occasion you may be allowed to sit on one of the seats bolted to the floor, and if you do you soon discover that you're probably more comfortable standing, thanks. The atmosphere in the waiting areas or anterooms away from staff is either boiling or freezing, kept at a constantly extreme temperature. It seems to switch to ensure that those who have access to alternative clothing options will always choose wrong. You think "I'll put this on, last time I was so cold in there." You go and it's burning hot and you can't take anything off. If you try to add or take off layers while inside, you'll always immediately be intercepted by the greeter. What you're doing is considered inappropriate behaviour in a public place and a reason to eject you and miss your slot. So what happens then? – you get more benefit.

Marks on the floor in places – bits of plastic stuck down, looks like years ago, any upgrade counted as an unnecessary cost – show routes to … somewhere. Maybe in those days you could find your way clearly round the place to see where you were going. Here and there, arrows, even a line of them going the same way, indicating a direction, one way, for example, but never all the way. No destination – at least not the one you had to get to.

You want to do it right, show willing and everything. It's for everyone to muck in, make it better. You want to get there, too, for your own safety. Following the paths they send you on, the paths they set out, blob, blob, blob, stay on the markers, this way, stay safe, keep your distance. But it doesn't make any sense. The dirt doesn't help, and the markers are torn or rucked up, faded till you can hardly see them, and there isn't any light coming in. The paths peter out, stop dead at closed doors, double back. Nothing goes nowhere.

You know you can't go back so you have to keep going on, towards you don't know what. Nothing to see ahead or to either side of you, and you'd think those big doors and ceilings being so high would give a sense of space. It just makes you feel small and scared all at the same time. You can't stretch, can't get a sense of where you are. Can't get any feel of the space you're in, can't think about it. Black holes and dark tunnels. Because then you might get to wondering how any person could have imagined this and designed it, and how did they make anyone build it. Not new, like they said. By the look of them you'd think the Central Houses are all ancient. That would never happen now. But the interior, the people who made it like that, what was the matter with them? You wonder how they could do it and where they ended up, what they went on to do. Down the trapdoors themselves, probably.

And there really are tunnels. It's not just crazy talk. They're real, so I've been told. Haven't seen them myself, but them who told me, they have. Seen them and walked in them, they say. They tell you this is a safe place to stay for you, don't have to come to Central House no more. Go forward, they say, you can't ever go back. And that's it.

Once was more than enough, they say. Not here, not where we have to go. Below the surface, they say. The tunnels are for their protection, so they have a safe route from their trains and cars into their offices here. So they don't see us or share common space. Or even air. Breathe the same air as us? — now that could really be dangerous. Of course they never touch you, and those screens between them and us at appointments, they're not glass. They can see us but we don't know what we're looking at – a reflection, a picture of someone else. Someone, somewhere, but not actually the face that you can see. That's a different job and we don't know if they can do both. You never see the same face twice but there's no knowing if the voice you hear and the face you see belong to the same person, or if either are from the person who is, in a loose sense of the word, communicating with you.

I often wonder, when I'm outside and walking the last 500 metres or so to Central, if they've made it so windy around the building on purpose. I don't know if it has to be like that. It's only wind, it's true, but you get badly buffeted about, almost knocked off your feet, as though the weather is playing a supporting role in the Conversion. Just another reminder that this is how it is, in case you were getting ideas. It's possible that it's accidental, temporary, unforeseen, the architect's lack of attention. It's possible that other places have come down or gone up and made it more windswept than it would otherwise have been or once was. But the level of detail, of what we know and of what we imagine, tells me no. They made it like that on purpose. It's pretty basic to work out what the wind will do when you're planning a building. Whether it was planned or not, it's a winner for them. We're led to believe they're forward-thinking and it's all part of their plan. A sorry state of affairs. Worse than that: not even sorry.

I've never been in a place like it. Bet everyone says that. From the outside it looks derelict, squatted maybe, except there's nothing hanging at the few windows, the ones that aren't bricked up. No sound, no lights either. But you know what's in there and have no choice but to go in. Once I've been in there a while, getting to where I have to go, I realise I can't even tell what floor I'm on. You hear something that sounds like lifts and distant footsteps. And you go on your way – I swear they move the walls round from week to week – to find the room you've been sent to. All on the same floor, no stairs, at least not anywhere in sight. On the way back, they send you out by a different door and you realise you've gone up a floor, or even two or three, without setting foot on a stair, without even seeing a staircase never mind a lift (as if). It's disorienting. Makes you feel unsafe, like you can't take care of yourself.

They send you different ways, though you still might end up in the same place. So, another route, when you thought there was only one. Nothing's ever made easy. Nothing can be taken for granted. On every occasion it's like another building entirely. One time I head off the way they sent me and I'm sure it takes me in a circle, right back to where I started. When I get there the lights are up, which they weren't before, and some chairs have been set out. Even so, I swear it's the same place. Chairs you'd be comfy in, almost begging you to sit down in them. And when did that last happen? One of the first times I go in there they're asking me questions in a tiny room. Barely enough space for three people and a table and me, although I don't know why it takes three of them to ask me a few simple questions when they already seem to know all the answers. With the room having such a high ceiling, it's like we're in a lift shaft, like the room is the wrong way up – supposed to be long and low-ceilinged. It's cold too, and very dusty.

So the measure is well strange, but the really odd thing about it is that in such a small room there are five doors. Five that I can see. It's possible there are even more behind me. And they aren't just doors leading to cupboards. Shuttling in and out all the time they are – the trustees, I think they're called – moving fast, obviously very busy, and in that space you can't do that without causing disruption. Every time it happens, someone has to move their chair, lean over, stand up, make way. A right old Piccadilly Circus, as they used to say.

When I was walking round this circle of corridors, I put my hand on the wall at one point. To steady myself. I'd come over dizzy. I forget you're not meant to touch anything. "Leave no trace," they say. Don't need no telling about that, but they tell and tell you all the same. My hand is all sweaty. And a bit mucky, it has to be said. So there's a mark. It's an accident. I saw it again the next time round. After that – how many minutes later I can't say – it was gone. Spooks you out because how do they know and how does someone get there to do that without you seeing or hearing them? And why bother, anyway? Don't know what that's about. Opened two doors. Expecting them to be locked. The first one, small and empty, funny smell that sends me straight back out again. The second deathly cold, like you've entered another country, and darker than the night ever is. For a while after that I'm not so interested in looking. None of it makes any sense and nothing is going to get any better, so what's the point anyway. Nothing good to find behind any of those doors.

If you know your way around down there, it's well worth the risk. That's part of the enjoyment. Yeah, it's a bit of a gamble, but being sure enough of the routes and the whys and wherefores, that's part of it. A real buzz you get. Some of that's because of being scared, sure, but it's not the main thing. But you do have to know what you're doing, otherwise it wouldn't be worth the risk. I'd never go by myself. I've looked at those maps, like we all have, but once I get down there it doesn't translate for me. And the danger is that I'll start following my so-called instinct, and that's not worth jack shit.

I can't be confident that I'd follow the routes. If you don't keep to them, you're really asking for it. That's what I was told by the guide I go with. There's a high risk. High payback. He isn't telling me every-thing – why would he? and who's paying him for it? – but he sketches it out in the dust, how there are two different levels of tunnels and mostly they're totally separate. In certain places, though, often at entry or exit points, the intersections need to be managed very carefully, what with echoes and dust and amplification. We use the deep tunnels, which is lucky, he reckons, because there's less chance of detection through noise on the surface. He also reckons the Coders don't really know about this other level, abandoned it when they decided to use the upper set. Forgot it. Out of sight, out of mind.

If there's a fall or a cave-in, he says, you've got no chance down there. On the upper level though, if that happens, they've put in safety walls and pillar reinforcements so people could survive, maybe. And it's less likely to happen in the first place. But most of the time the tunnels are still the best chance for easy escape. At some point they'll find out about this, too, and that'll be that. People live down there and everything, he says. Hardly any bodies ever need to be recovered. Strange, that. If there ever is a takeover bid, he says, there are plans. Anyone still down there, they'll be left to the rats or drowned in concrete poured through the hatch.

Looking up doesn't happen that much. Eyes on the ground, for all sorts of reasons. Best to be careful. When you do look up, almost nothing sits on the windowsills or hangs behind window frames. Maybe nothing at all. No plants, no curtains or blinds. Strict rules apply – it all has to be straight, precise. Even if you think you see stuff, no knowing what it is. Some windows look like mirrored glass but they're not, it's just light catching the glass. Windy, of course. Pigeons suspiciously absent. Likewise seagulls. A no-fly zone. Cats and dogs have been cleansed from the streets too (high time, to my mind).

Reading a plan [Code archive material, from files] Fixed hatches. Staircases that go nowhere. Door mechanisms with no handles. Rooms with double-height sections for maximum temperature and acoustic affect. Blank windows and door apertures bricked-up for textural interest. "Brief," it says at the top. Blind passageways, hinged walls, fake partitions, windowless cubicles, decoy stairways. A hidden staircase to the basement. Trapdoors leading to dark places. Sealed rooms. No light, no windows. Multiple dummy doors. Cupboards leading into walkways, and hidden doorways opening on to cupboards.

Who needs to know their way around? Separation from any other units in the building for ultimate processing performance, a completely over-arching system. "The frontage divided by eight windows across, with separated vertical steel dividers running down the building. At the summit, narrow apertures run vertically, housing a gallery or greenhouse, with two of the masonry sections equalling the width of the windows on the lower floors." Who cares about any of that? Hmm, high investment strategy. "Unexpected and unusual directions," the handout says. Interesting. Heating sources – brick structures like kilns. A chute slicked with axle grease from second floor to basement. A lightable gas jet, controlled remotely. A second basement for storage of sensitive or perishable material, temperature-controlled. Airtight. Metal-clad walls. Empty vats embedded in floors. That's more like it.

You don't want to even think about what this might be planning for. Likewise with the walk-in vault, air- and sound-tight spaces and asbestos walls, the deadspace, full of corners where light can't penetrate. Stale air. Not everyone knows about all this. And what's the use of knowing now – why would you want to?

Purpose-built, that's what I heard. But designed to look otherwise. What did they used to call that again? Quack architecture? Function is all. The building itself is nothing. It's enforcement by design, that's what I'm saying. Coercitecture. There's no one there to tell you if you get lost. You consider yourself told because there's no other way to go. Have to keep your head down to see where you're going. It's inside but it's like being outdoors, where you have to watch where you're walking in case you trip over stones or branches. So you carry on, looking down for the most part, certainly not standing tall. From the first moment when you look up – probably the only time that happens – and see that giant archway, you're in their power. We're talking The Big Man here. Keep you in your place. Do this, go there, walk that way. You'll be on the floor before you get round the first corner. Like a fairground house of horrors and hall of mirrors combined, you've got no idea where you are.

People who overuse their benefit or who access what they're not supposed to access never come out of the building. They push them through those cupboards that lead to other rooms, and then at the end into a room with a trapdoor or a big open chimney. That's what they say. You'll finally be warm at least. Yes, that's what they say. A threat or a promise – no idea which it is.

It's the building that tells you all you need to know. Doesn't need to tell you, really. It's obvious. There's no another option. This goes one way and you're on it, mate. Which is why they don't need to have people there to say it to you directly. It's all laid out, and that's the route. The way it is, there's no knowing whether others get sent on other routes. Or even if there are other routes. We can't describe them to each other, not even if we had enough capacity, and no one does these days. It's Full Recovery for all of us soon, no getting away from it. We can't describe them because there's nothing memorable – and even if we could remember something about the route, how could we say it? From visit to visit there's no recognition. It's bland and dull and mucky. Bad lighting. Bit of a smell. Could be anywhere. And there was always one of them to say how the smell is most likely coming from us.

Time is slow in the waiting room. Nothing to look at or listen to, no windows to gaze out of and never anyone else to talk to. It's no talking, anyway. Feels as though time is crawling backwards. Once there was a clock there that was impossibly slow. The time it showed was before you'd even left the house to get to Central. Could be an issue about battery replacement, maybe, or just someone mucking about. There are one or two other clocks, and sometimes they're there, sometimes not. You'd swear they've all been fast-forwarded so you think you're late on arrival. If you're lucky, the lengthy wait is all the punishment you'll get for your failure. If not, it's deletion time. But often you can't tell what time it is anyway because you're not getting any light in from outside.

Wait for what? Waiting for nothing. Waiting for who knows. Waiting for a continuation and retrenchment of uncertainty. Waiting to catch it. Waiting for something you don't want. Waiting for it. Emptiness. No sounds. No passing footfall. No alerts or rings or hums. Dead space – so you might be dead too. No way of knowing. Tea? Oh, funny ... yeah, that old joke. "Thank you for asking. May I have a cup of Earl Grey while I'm waiting?" Really, as if. Uncomfortable furniture is all you'll get, dirty, small, at a great height or too close to the ground. Not even any signage telling you what not to do. Not necessary. What not to do is anything at all.

This is how buildings call the shots. Hold sway over your every footstep. You go through the arch, the gate, whatever, and abandon hope, as if hope were still a thing. You are not – ever! – welcome here. You are not welcome. This is not for you. This is to you, on you. This building is a sensory assault course, one you will never complete because that is its intention. It's designed to floor you, to overwhelm you with difficulty. It's not supposed to inspire you with the resolve to do better next time, until you beat this thing. It is not for beating. You, on the other hand, are beaten – that's a given! It's your fundamental state, which this building communicates to you instantly, clearly, by its powerful silence.

Designed to provoke the maximum feelings of discomfort, failure, insignificance on every level – materials, colour, texture, circulation, location, ventilation, lighting. It works exceptionally well. As she said, no one believed that architecture could be this powerful. Who'd have thought it? These architects know their business. Oh, they know what they're doing, that lot.

You may suspect that there are other people in the building, but you don't know. Or maybe you know they are there but not who they are or what they do. Fear of the unknown works best. It is the absence of the possibility of knowing that causes the fear. That's their most effective weapon. That and the endless repeat. You have to keep going there or go outlaw. That's not much of a choice. For some, it makes more sense to do what you can from this side, though it's precious little. Unless you're going to join those Wall-Es.

3. Monumental Systems

Central House/s: The Place for Alpha

"A has had its day," they say. Now for a new beginning. We are fully engaged in how to establish the best possible responses to the changes the units will be experiencing at whatever benefit level. We will work through options and possibilities, always, and here are the results in built form. Central House/s is a symbol of our achievement, literally set in stone.[36] It frees up the improvident use of premises decreed necessary to house and deliver the old system. We are now unveiling the specially adapted locations, our portfolio of Central House/s, to welcome recipients and respond to their needs at graduated intervals. This is an exciting project, exploring new ways of using old spaces: maximum interventionary gain at minimum cost. In this and many other ways the system's attributes mirror its delivery mechanisms right across the board. Clearly, the investment application is broad in order to ensure success; also to guarantee economy across physical premises and extensive refits, training for staff and management, and a rollout of completely redesigned systems machinery, administrative environments and materials.

The building is a monument to the system and a marker of it, or, more appropriately, a series of markers. It is extremely important that the fleet of Central House/s reflects our values in terms of how they work and look: function, form, style, as advised. Given the gravity of what we're undertaking, a classic style is appropriate: the depth, the solidity, the impact it will have over decades if not centuries. Further-

36 On some sites, where stone was not used due to availability and cost issues, specially clad breeze blocks were substituted.

more, because The Hardship threatens to tarnish the gleaming achievements of the Code, we must distance ourselves from it. A new strain of optimism is what's needed. Although we avoid the abhorrent so-called modern, nonetheless ours is an ultramodern response to a current problem, albeit one that has dogged us, loomed over us, for decades. What is required is a fittingly contemporary response, an innovative take on a classical theme. It's known as the re-neo-classical, as we've been given to understand, and it signifies an architecture that is substantial, imposing, beautiful and, above all, fit for purpose.

•

"Located on the top three floors of this landmark building, Vantage Point offers prestigious serviced office space through contractual leases. The stunning 360° views of the city (arguably none better!) provide the perfect backdrop for creative thinking and the entrepreneurial spirit. With naturally lit meeting rooms and high-specification facilities that provide an energising minimalist interior, this distinctive office suite is the perfect combination of space and purpose."

Additional to the real estate pitch above:
Where services ("public benefit", yawn yawn) are still operational, they are confined to the lowest floors of the building and have their own circulation routes, egress/ingress, hosting services, etc.

Sold off and rented back on lease.[37] Built over transport. Below, strictly controlled, safe and easy access to the tunnels.

**Ideal – acquire soonest. The Vantage Point floors are ideal

37 Short-term commitment, more expensive: confirmed as good business practice and procedure to make public services appear more expensive and, once budgets had been cut further, ineffective.

for us blue-sky thinkers. For the trustee grunts the lower levels will do.

•

This is The Place. This is what I always imagined it to be. For the space alone I would work here for nothing. But our work is so very, very important – that's what they told me at interview, and the longer I'm here the more I know it to be true. And to safeguard our wellbeing they've made sure we are shielded from unpleasant exterior realities. Such thoughtfulness! They said that because of its importance, the environment in which we work had to be to an unusually high standard. That's putting it mildly: it is absolutely gorgeous! You can only admire their commitment and honesty.

The importance of our delivery environment reflects the difficulties of what we have to do. Yes, we spend time in actual meetings with the Gifted. Actually, it's not quite like that. The functionality of the hangout spaces is such that on the other side – the fourth wall, if you like – the Gifted are led to believe we're physically there in the room with them. Uh-uh. Not so, that would be most undesirable. Great care is taken to keep us safe, especially when more than one of us – trustees, I mean – is in the space (overlapping image projections can make the Gifted realise we're not there in person). Seriously though, I should be paying them to let me work here. Talk about a free lunch!

•

Missive from Inhouse AlphaCode Architectural Advisors

The building is described officially as a community space. It hosts a multitude of activities and uses and develops its pro-gramme according to shifting patterns of occupation and new functions as they emerge. This is in addition or along-side the teaching and training functions, the benefit offices and related public areas, and finally the education rooms where intensive reminder sessions for the Gifted of the advantages of their benefits are undertaken. Retreats, they're termed. Naturally, this means that access is pro-vided according to individual need and status – not every-one enjoys the same level of entitlement. We must also always thank users for their patience given that updates and refurbishments will be taking place almost continuously.

Lighting levels vary according to an algorithmic system designed by our providers. This is a special, groundbreaking tariff that has been developed with a multitude of uses in mind. It is considered pleasing for the Gifted to be able to experience this creative lighting during their time with us as an additional and not insignificant benefit, one that can inspire a thoughtful, creative response. Circulation and layouts have been designed in line with the most recent and relevant scien-tific principles, factored to the number of appointments, fre-quency, time of day, etc. Routes are allotted according to levels of challenge, inspiration and achievement, then on a random basis for flexibility and variation. The withdrawal of routine – the abolition of the expected – raises the educational bar, both for trustees and those receiving benefit. Physical fitness as well as fitness for purpose are the foundational principles of the spatial design across the Central House/s group. While non-singular, as noted earlier, the architecture of each Central House/s is nonetheless known as the "single exemplar". Although the building's anonymity is not crucial, we do not want to depart from the monumental, so each Central House/s advertises itself with its glowering presence.

To save money, many of the Central House/s have been

equipped with items from closing schools, and seating areas are kitted out in the bright primary colours more often associated with children. These cheery colours are also selected with the intention of lifting the spirits in what are challenging circumstances for all. However, the size of the chairs thwarts any expectation of comfort or rest while awaiting appointments. People are kept on their toes, literally and figuratively. There are, unaccountably, those who still find reason to complain about the facilities. What can I say? There's simply no pleasing some people.

Those who are too large to sit – or are otherwise, for whatever reason, unable to mobilise themselves to enter – are considered to be creating their own circumstances of unavailability. These units are clearly timewasters who feel their pitiful individual desires deserve special consideration. Let's be clear: none shall be given! Potential benefits will be reassessed until suitable adjustments have been made. Any demonstration of inflexibility on the part of the units is unacceptable and will be reflected in their benefit level.

•

From: Trustee Appraisal/Feedback #2

You must already have heard that, from the outside, Central House/s is nothing special to look at. Huge and anonymous – that's what they say. Still stuck in The Hardship fallout. But that just tells me they don't get it. Never seen it from the outside, myself, so who's to know? Inside, well that's another matter. The redesign for AlphaCode was integral to the programme. What I mean is, they didn't come up with the strategy and then look for office space to use. The Central House/s are part of it – of the strategy, I mean. All part and parcel of the same thing. A bit of joined-up thinking that really does the business.

It's a pleasure to be here in the building and a pleasure to operate the programme. Absolutely! You really feel that all the stops have been pulled out to make a success of it. And it works big time. This is a comfortable, spacious, well lit environment, and it has all the amenities you could possibly wish for. Everything we could possibly need has been provided, and then some. Plenty of jokes with colleagues about never wanting to leave. Well, nobody will be leaving this job, not voluntarily, that's for sure. And where else is there to go? Nowhere that could better this.

Those workspaces, they're like gaming stations. It's a fairytale. It's all about creativity, designed so we can be our best selves, do our best work, giving the Gifted the best, most perfectly considered service. Now who feels gifted!

In what they call the "front-facing spaces", they've used screens that allow us to see the units, whereas the units see someone they think is us. Avatar, is it? A kind of digital superimposition. A safety measure, for our protection, so there's no face-to-face contact and therefore no chance of them passing on germs and viruses, fleas and lice. Absolutely no chance. We're not going to meet any of them outside of Central, are we? I mean, how could that happen? Or where? We don't go to any of the places they go. But even so, them upstairs have got a point about us not taking risks.

Oh yes, the experience of being in Central House/s is like this for the Gifted too. I mean, no question. We've all heard the talk about them queuing to get in and trying to hide so they can stay the night. Everything is delivered for their benefit, that's what AlphaCode is about. The only difference is that their entrance is a different one to ours, and that's a security issue.

•

Upgrade of Central House/s – draft report

There's no avoiding the symbolism of the high and low, the upper level and the downside, the masters' and the servants' quarters, above and below stairs. But why would anyone want to avoid it? It's a mark of both achievement and ambition. The top floor is, so I've heard, glazed on all sides, floor-to-ceiling walls of glass offering an unparalleled "vantage point" (which happens to be the audacious new name of the building) on the city below. That's what we'll be occupying very soon. But "Advantage" might have been a better choice of name, taking it to the next level, assuming that's even possible.

In between are several brise-soleils, or an approximation of them, to deflect sunlight. You can also see how the tower would itself impede the sun falling on certain areas below. Fair enough; why should those down there benefit from it? The door for the Gifted is on the perpetually shady side. The upper levels are contained, neat in their exterior and interior. Seen from below, the sole indications of occupancy are items leaning against the inside of windows, causing brighter areas on the glass. It's not what it seems: these are reflections from boxy fluorescent light fittings. But when you look again, you see there are so many layers to those windows, the double (or triple?) glazing, the screens, the secondaries. Whatever they are, no one would easily be able to see in or out. With so many layers of glass, transparency isn't multiplied; instead, it distorts and shields, and that's probably the point of it. Privacy is always paramount.

From: Trustee Appraisal/Feedback #3
Note: access still above ground for CH/2 at this stage

On the plaza outside Central are arrangements of granite blocks, the same surface area as the paving stones but of diverse heights and depths. They form a varied excrescence, as though erupting from below ground. In earlier times this would have been an ideal place to sit, watch the world go by, and dream – that's how the marketing copy would have it. People would compete to sit on blocks with a bit of shade from the plane trees dotted illiberally around the plaza. In summer, a perfect place to catch a few rays while eating lunch.

And then there's the glass ceiling over part of the street. It must have been warmer with the glass overhead, although there was no insulation as such, only the considerable warmth of money changing hands, the heat of exchange wrought by shopping and retail management. A kind of inside/outside space – you felt inside but you could see the outside world. Above that: the open-air balcony. Incredibly, the remains of an old sign suggests that it was open access too. Hard to believe. Think of all the trouble it would cause – people climbing up, out of hours, and even jumping off!

•

HMRC#00015 Property Management – draft 3

Central House/s brings a solid physical dimension to the AlphaCode, which in its abstractions and theoretical rigour would otherwise be too much for many units to grasp. It's simple: they come because they have to, so we can monitor obedience and see that they're sticking to the programme. The more often they come, the higher the benefit. Central House/s offers a safe haven, a place and a time in which they can have every confidence their needs will be met.

We couldn't take their situation any more seriously, nor examine it more minutely – every letter, every unit. How are they managing their letter allocation? Is it hurting? Do they need more? Demonstrably we want the best for all units, the highest possible rates of benefit they can be prescribed. We adjust the benefit quickly to suit changing circumstances. Without the mass of resources in Central House/s, this would be unachievable. Frequent appointments keep the units on the move, stopping them from getting stuck – well, we try – in awkward situations brought about by inappropriate social mixing and the chatterboxing that tends to ensue. How dangerous that can be for even the most mealy-mouthed of them; wasteful of their benefit. It's strongly to be discouraged, especially given the longwinded stories they're inclined to tell.

Coming in to make their declarations about use and attendant hardships provides the impetus they often lack to go back out and utilise their new entitlement in the best way possible. We provide stimulus and add variety to their schedule, which now that they have been freed from the burden of assignments can become dull and undifferentiated. It also keeps them off the streets, apparently, although we don't know this firsthand. The appointments create an ongoing record of their behaviour, and of the simple truth of AlphaCode – that we always do the right thing for the right reason. Despite which, sadly, some units don't always see the joy in their benefit. But we do what we can.

Access to most of the Central House/s is at street level. There's only one certified route, but the tunnels have more, and that's not helpful because underground routes encourage illicit behaviours of various kinds, including secrets being shared and lies being told. We need to keep the units on track. But there are always some who won't knuckle under. With all the other underpasses and walkways in the city, high and low, it is a risk to open up the units to such extended possibilities of movement and mixing, but for the moment the advantages of having multiple certified routes outweigh the risks.

In Central itself, it's a much more complex matter than different doors. Call it what you will: apartheid, concentration camps, segregated education, trade entrance, boys' and girls' playgrounds, public/employees, Lords and Ladies' toilets, etc. Effectively, users are presented with singular buildings but different access points according to their status. "Access all areas" is nonsense, a clear category error. One would have thought that the levels of deterrence currently in force would be sufficient to make users fearful of transgression or even curiosity. Apparently not. There will always be those who will risk everything to stray from their designated path and entrance; they just can't help themselves.

Single-route traffic is the only way to maintain regulatory safety standards. In establishing Alpha-compliant distance codes, the audits confirm beyond doubt that the substantial majority of units are incapable of following guidance or meeting requirements. Indeed, data from watchers and other more covert sources make it abundantly clear that an inability to comply is, sadly, the norm. Hence the need for continual benefit increases. Considerable resources – record levels of funding, in particular – were allocated to innovative wayfinding methods. AlphaCode values the details as well as the big picture. It is only with this comprehensive focus that we can be certain our system is watertight, airtight, and fit for purpose.

Later we'll address in detail the question of dress codes in Central House/s, but for now it's worth emphasising one important factor: that whatever is worn must be appropriate to both the space inhabited and the role enacted and that safety for all is the main concern. With safety in mind, the spatial design for the interiors of each of the Central House/s has been ordered in such a way that danger through proximity is avoided. We appreciate the high level of risk inherent in the work done at contact level by our trustees and other operatives, given the unitary propensity to indulge in psychological and emotional outbursts.[38] In regular security incidents and "situations", as we call them, any liquid expulsion from mouth or eyes must immediately be reported. In such high-alert circumstances, the guilty unit must be ejected, the trustee decontaminated and in most cases quarantined.

Likewise, any skin contact, whether accidental or not, is deemed an act of violence and must be responded to with the robust self-defense measures learned in your training sessions. To help keep contact to a bare minimum, the recent introduction of projected avatars and, in some cases, lifelike robots is continuing apace. We can all look to a future where those of us still subject to threats from unstable and/or dangerous units never has to face them or be near them, unshielded, unpartitioned, ever again.

Some of you may be aware that there have been attempts at other times and in other places to make spatial separation work, usually on the basis of race, religion, colour, culture. In several cases such measures were instigated as founding principles. And while they were indeed highly principled and, in many cases, also very rewarding for those on the right side of the divide, ultimately they failed. Some were met with levels of unrest that today we are unfamiliar with. "Fail again, fail better" was then a saying, trite and fatuous though it was. We, however, are not failing. Nor do we have any intention of failing. Our system is finely calibrated and, as we are continually reminded by the gorgeous silence, it could hardly work better.

•

38 We appreciate that this may be genetically led.

We all have fears about tunnel terrorism. When the programmer came, he said it was understandable and that anyone who could not put those fears behind them should contact him once he'd finished speaking. Because no one ever will, he's seen to have been effective across the board. There is no terrorist threat, no cause for concern – that's the official line. Even so, among friends, or at least among those we believe we can trust, we discuss our fears and even big them up. Everyone wants to be The One worst affected/ most panicked/having the least sleep yet frequent nightmares/with lost appetite/feeling desperate/without strategies or hope. What we lack in our lives is drama. We're desperate to show each other what a terrible time we're having, how there's no way out, no way forward, yet we remain, against all the odds, stoic.

The Gifted think they've got it bad. (Huh. We might even claim that ourselves. With close associates only, obvs). But even if they feel the situation is bad, they follow a track that someone else has laid out for them. All they have to do is follow it. It's an easy life and a simple one. And let's be clear: I don't begrudge them. I know it's only right that those less able have to receive a high level of benefit. And for those who aren't just less able but can't, who really absolutely can't, there's recovery. It's win-win for the Gifted, no doubt about it. The likes of us, though, we have to appear measured and in control at all times.

Many of the units … it's really quite sad … they don't get it, not at all. We provide them with a peaceful ambience, an ideal environment, in a public building in which people are helped in the most comforting manner possible. But all they do is carp about dim lighting! So many styles of seating laid out for them – they don't like that either. You'd think they'd have learned to welcome stuff that's so far out of their league. But no, it seems they want the usual rubbish. It's a damned shame. And before you know it, some of the team start to say that benefit's a waste of scarce resources and pitched too high for the human garbage we serve. Personally I don't agree, but there's plenty who'll voice opinions like that given half a chance. It's strictly against the spirit of our custom and training, and if those upstairs get to hear about it *they'll get promoted*. No no no, that's not even funny. I don't know where that came from. Please don't report that. What I meant was: they'll get terminated. No more work. Won't see them here anymore – or anywhere else, for that matter.[39]

They knew what they were doing by reusing these buildings. You can't help but wonder whether they were trying to keep people in or keep them out. Who knows if any of those layers were removable, or movable at all. It wasn't for noise insulation, though. There was nothing in there that would disturb anyone. The opposite, if anything. "Quiet enough to wake the dead" – isn't that what they used to say? So it wasn't soundproofing, was it? Unless the point was to keep the noise from travelling outwards. At first you couldn't help but wonder what was going on in there, and then you decided not to. Someone said that the glass ceiling was to catch people as they fell, to stop the bodies from landing on the ground. But you never even see them looking out, much less climbing out and jumping. I heard it only happened at night, anyway, and the leap ... it wasn't always by choice. But who knows.

---

39 The trustee in question has now been placed on indefinite leave.

Reflected in itself – what's that called, then? Architectural narcissism? The front entrance could hardly be less welcoming if it were bricked up or had a "closed" sign nailed to a door of rusty corrugated iron. Whatever you want to call it, public it is not. The security guard [rather: the welcome delegate] doesn't even speak, just shakes his head.[40] It's not all bad, though. Think of everything we get: transport and easy access ... and the safety tunnels. It's not just the job. Imagine how it would be if we didn't have all that at our disposal. It would be dangerous for our health, if nothing else. You'd never know who you were rubbing shoulders with, and you really can't be too careful.

Back to reality. These days, on a mid-autumn afternoon, the spaces outside are abandoned, filthy, and unpleasantly weathered. A handful of small evergreens shaped into cones and spirals sit in planters, looking cheap and stunted. The "privlic space experience", as it's known. Don't sit don't loiter don't lie down don't rest. Don't stay too long, obvs, or do anything that might draw the attention of the guards lurking in the shade. Best not do anything they might want to stop you from doing.

•

HMRC#45 – policy doc

The organisational structure of AlphaCode is mirrored in the organisation of the buildings, in the designation of areas, floors, levels and, naturally, lifts for the specific use of certain groups and categories of employee. Each of the

40 Note: institute wage bonus there.

41 None of the Central House/s are newbuilds, although appearances can be deceiving. "Refurbishment", as it was once known, while still costly, was considered to be a more effective use of funds; it's also less noticeable than new towers and changed landscapes.

buildings was selected because its structure would facilitate such a mapping of territories.[41] To each their own and to everyone their needs – that's the ethos underpinning the system; as true for the benefit roll-out as it is for the allocation of space in the building. Those engaged in developing and producing schema naturally need time and space in which to do so effectively; requirements that have been met literally and metaphysically.

Their daily work and various longer-term goals are informed by their views of distant streets and the units far below, at street level – all of which can easily be seen from their vantage point on the top three floors. Housed as they are, at the apex of their building, they can observe and study the fabric of the city and the wretched conditions and circumstances that bear on their work, all of which serves to remind them of their onerous responsibilities. The housing of the Alpha-Code Conversion in the towers is a deliberate tactic involving strategy, policy and delivery, aside from any architectural aesthetic or preference intrinsic to the project.

Moving down the House/s: Those engaged in delivering this work, in operating the system at "the coalface" – the interface, if you like, between the creed of ministerial wisdom and the trustees who benefit from it and deliver it to the units – have a strikingly different work rhythm to those on the top floor. Contact between the different levels is therefore stringently avoided due to fears that intermingling could interrupt productivity and pose a potential security hazard. Speed, efficiency and accuracy are requirements that all applicants must demonstrate. Although the shifts for those at the lower levels are long and intense, they believe that they enjoy good work conditions, and on a relative and appropriate level they do. They have a grid and a script, both of which they follow, as it were, to the letter. Nothing is left unresolved or to chance. Nothing is allowed to be unsatisfactory.

A degree of explanation is required here with regard to lifts bearing numbers for which passes are required. The first lift must be used only by those whose offices are located at the very top of the building; this is true of all Central House/s. It is important to maintain a strict separation between the delivery operatives, or trustees as they are now called, and the officers of conception.[42] The "officers of delivery", as they term themselves, only need to know what has to be delivered, and this is represented spatially in their provision of rooms and their access to them.[43]

Two further lifts serve floors 1 to 25 and 26 to 29. The official line is that this segregation of lifts has been done for technical architectural reasons only. As mentioned a little earlier, a tall building with a single continuous shaft is infrastructurally weaker than one having two shafts. But the avoidance of intermingling is important too: a vital aspect of social engineering. Who knows what happens on those other floors? "Not my Business" is the desired response, although "Who cares?"might be more common. In a further example of social engineering, the contained and limited access to the shopping and leisure facilities below gives the impression of an unthreatening space open to all.[44] Glass canopies projecting over and across the thoroughfare likewise extends the look and feel, however false, of transparency and openness.

42 On some level mirroring the separation between trustee and Gifted, but even more crucial in that the delivery of the system must be kept separate from the possibility of any post-rollout intervention by its inventors.

43 Not to be explained in this way publicly, but it is analogous to the Gifted being told only what benefit they will receive, not how it has been calculated. Discussion of any kind is superfluous. Also, the grunts must be encouraged to believe that their work is extremely important, even while progress renders their role less and less meaningful.

44 To extend this effect, shops currently boarded up will receive inducements to reopen.

Transportation hubs can be accessed by all staff using separate routes to exit the building.[45] For those whose work requires it, limited access is provided to disused railway tunnels below transport facilities. Like the provision of separate doors for unit safety, lifts are only accessible on the Code side of the House/s, invisible from both exterior and interior to those who aren't permitted to use them (and who needn't even know they're there). The ambit of specificity of the building is such that for different users it is, in effect, a different building. Qualities of shelter, comfort or fitness have been taken into account and kitted out beyond normal considerations. This is, after all, the future: innovative architecture taken to giddy heights. More levelling up from which we may take a certain satisfaction.

45 We are engaged in efforts to fulfill this goal at CH/2; currently access at trustee level involves exiting to the exterior. Appropriate safety provision is in place until the matter is resolved.

4. Strategic Treatise

In this section, the retrieved documents give starker insights into ATax. It gets harder to swallow, more painful to read. The writers, still anonymous (though some papers are initialled or coded), have begun to talk more freely, apparently secure in the knowledge that their strategies and treatises (and whatever other nonsense titles they gave their corporate hate speech) are perfectly acceptable. Indeed, they seem confident that what they're doing is universally welcome and of great value.

They kept records. The worse ones, authoritarian regimes and despots, always do. Material evidence to show they'd followed the science and their hardline tactics were fully justified. Boxes and boxes of it. Many drafts of the same text, all neatly organised and cross-referenced down the years. At first, anyway. They were obsessed with systems and efficiency and documentation, and that held true until the final, chaotic days when the scheme was collapsing and papers were piled high and in great disorder. Thousands of documents were stuffed in desk drawers, in overflowing bins, and scattered sometimes inches deep across the floor. Not just in offices and other work spaces; in lifts and corridors; kitchen areas and bathrooms too.

In truth, their so-called system amounted to little more than self-deception, fakery, lies and deceit. But we fell for it, and hard. While searching through the papers they left behind, we weeded out the following selections in an attempt to make sense and give a taste of what the ethos of the Code was all about. Read it and weep. Despite their confusion and self-contradiction, the documents nonetheless allow us to reach a broad understanding of what underpinned the Alphabet Tax, as well as how, in all its cruelty, it was imposed and implemented, and how finally it fell apart.

Scrabble, a game that originated long ago, in pre-Hardship times, consists of a random delivery of the same number of letters to each person in a group of players.[46] Each player is given seven letters with which to form words. The letters have different "scores" according to their value as allotted by the game's designers. The letters in most frequent use – the commonly used ones, the Es, Ts, and so on – give low scores. There are also blanks, which, not having a letter printed on them, score zero, though they can be used to stand in for any letter required to make a word.

So far so curious, the pastimes of old, making play of such dangerous materials. The distribution of letters, though, is interesting in relation to our regime, as it involves a system whose admirable even-handedness we consider worth emulating. While many of the common letters are supplied liberally, so that each player is likely to have some of them fairly often, thus facilitating their play, only a small number of less frequently used letters is supplied. Why? Because these are the letters that appear in far fewer words. Scarcity scores in this game, and these letters, more difficult to include in words, score highly.

Obviously our work is not a game. The rules of Scrabble are not something we would adopt wholesale. To put it another way that relates to the project in hand: far fewer of certain letters are supplied because they are not necessary for the players to make words. There is, therefore, no real need for those letters. If one follows it through, that's the logical standpoint of Scrabble. Who really needs those letters? Here's where it begins to have real meaning for us, to have a possi-

46 "Random" and "same" are obviously antithetical to our conceptual basis – bear with us, nonetheless.

ble Code value. Those uncommon letters exist only to up the ante. But as I say, our work is not a game: high scores in our work relate to our performance in devising the Code's systems of governance which guide the units to better letter use and increase the numbers of the Recovered.[47]

As already stated, different letters have different scores, and the letters least used have the highest scores. Blanks score zero. The player who scores the most, by creating words with the highest scoring letters that are placed strategically on the highest scoring parts of the board, wins. Winning is largely down to skill, not luck, and our logistians and statisticians factored this understanding into the science of the AlphaCode.

The Gifted's "score" is meticulously assessed according to need, incorporating present circumstances and an expert prediction of future requirements. Simply put: What is it that needs to be said and how can it be achieved with the least burden, i.e. with the fewest letters? Perhaps the most dynamic aspect of our project is that it is not about imposing restrictions on the units and limiting their expectations. Rather, it is about enabling and helping them; about removing unnecessary and unfair expectations to expedite an equitable, shared effect. It is also about rewards not penalties, correction not punishment, emancipation not bondage. We are all in this together, though clearly we are not all the same and not all of us are capable of shouldering exactly the same letter load. To each their own. Or, put another way: some of us can score highly without letters, whereas others really shouldn't be in the game at all.

Rumours abound about staff using the term "scrabble" as some kind of jargon, or perhaps even swear word. While we

47 Any decrease is unacceptable.

deplore that kind of glibness, evidencing as it does an approach and attitude that can only be described as unprofessional, there is no reason to disparage the system of distribution accorded this name. Indeed, it can be appreciated for its clarity and simplicity.

Scrabble is, after all, only a game, but one that has been around for generations, and the reason it has endured is because of how adaptable it is to changes in language usage. This flexibility is true also of The AlphaCode, which guarantees an ever-quieter future as increasing numbers of units reach full recovery year on year.

•

Trustee Knowledge Alert
*top level security clearance only *******

There are concerns about the number of trustees asking questions about the data from the recorders, watchers, influencers and snitchers, and how this data segues with benefit entitlement assessment. They must never know that there is no such data or that benefit levels have no grounding in assessment. They must continue to be told that the system is complex, groundbreaking and flawless in operation, and that for reasons of security access to such information is limited. In most circumstances, the threat of being removed from their privileged position will stifle such awkward enquiries. There is also anecdotal evidence from Central House/s suggesting that some trustees are becoming publicly dismissive of the security-level separations policy, saying that it hides the absence of a system rather than addresses security hierarchy issues. Such cases need to be referred to unit re-education sites.

Whereas strategists and senior Coders are kept separate from each other in their workspaces, the same can't always be said of the units. As they make their way to an appointment at Central House/s (the only time they're allowed out of doors), there's always the chance they'll encounter another of their kind and start a conversation. This is unacceptable and potentially dangerous. One solution to the problem would be for trustees to deliver unit slots throughout the night as well as during daytime, thereby significantly reducing the number of units on the street at any one time.

•

Case Study – audio transcript

> [fade in]
> If you say that, you lose a C.
>> What's that? Like, you see?
> It's a C! You know, for cup and coat. C for cat.
>> Oh, all right. Give it a rest. Whatever. Don't
>> know. Don't have that, then.
> What about S, you still got that? Sweet shoe shop sugar ...
> [fade]

In the above exchange between an interviewer and his interviewee, they aren't playing a word game, it's real life. This is our new world, where unit access to letters for the lucky majority is controlled and closely monitored. With super-generous entitlements across the board at all levels, the system of benefit is tailored to avoid overburdening them or straining resources to allow efficient communication. Units assessed as fit to use letters receive an allowance that correlates with their condition and their level of need. And in this new life, if units don't get the letters, they can't speak. They are then free to go quietly about their business and enjoy their new-found freedom. An additional benefit is that they also have no need to write, and if they can't write they're excused from education because, really, to be blunt about it, there's no point. It would be an added, unfair encumbrance, an unnecessary worry. Only those who've had a thorough education can access a full set of letters.[48]

Others – by which I mean those who have achieved a certain level of giftedness – have access to officially licensed outlets that can equip them with extra resources. Education is for those who need it and who will make something of it in terms of bringing their knowledge into public service to aid efficient communication. This is the only path to allocation. Benefit cannot be bought – that's the point. It is free to all, but only the named recipient can use it. Each recipient has a minutely calibrated and individualised allocation. Letters are not for sharing!

Roots: The AlphaConversion
*security level ****
An Internal History

In the wake of The Hardship, an immediate response was required to restore order on the streets. The riots and attempts at insurrection had to be quashed, once and for all. What we came up with, the shutdown, or Big Quiet as it was known in some quarters, was a revelation. Although it was introduced as a stop-gap, to get the rioters back indoors, it made us see its potential value for the future of our society. The point was – and forever is – that the quiet could be more than a tempo-rary measure to allow us time to prepare for post-Hardship realities. Quiet could be fundamental to turning our lives around by focusing on what matters most: Us.

As I'm speaking to colleagues and allies here, I know I can be frank. Those initial extensions of shutdown were intro-

48 It is intrinsic to the system that the notion of a "full set" of letters has a fluidity involving a number of interpretations, each according to the iden-tity of the intended recipient.

duced purely to buy time. But they also gave us time to realise the truth, which was that shutdown had the capacity to deliver everything we wanted, the perfect combination of factors in which to get the Conversion set in place. It was time to stop this nonsense of providing a platform to all and sundry, of equal levels of provision, on the false assumption that we are all the same. At a stroke we'd sweep away the tedious debates and endless complaints and restore a substantial part of the capital and revenue that had been lost in The Hardship. We knew that it would take time and that it would require careful, extensive planning. What we didn't know at the time was what world-beating planners we'd turn out to be.

Letter by letter, week by week, we'd close down the units until we'd reached the ultimate goal of hearing only what we wanted to hear: informed, rational debate framed by us and among ourselves. Sure, we had the initial expense of refurb and equipping Central House/s, as well as those gophers, the watchers and the trustees, but it was all done economically, to a very tight budget, though not everyone was party to that. Cue much publicised distress over budgetary constraints. What we got was, in fact, cheap at the price, and what we saved in terms of actual budgets came in very handy, thank you. Unsurprisingly, the units didn't help themselves, what with their increasingly limited powers of expression and lifelong poor communication skills. Thanks for those, too!

For many years we'd been trying to shut the units down but hadn't quite worked out how to go about it. But circumstances changed, and much to our advantage. Even before shutdown, any semblance of regulatory authority overseeing our plans had long gone, so essentially we were unmonitored. It took us a while to grasp how much slack we had and how far we could go with it. We'd been too caught up in thinking we had to create a completely integrated foolproof system. But the response to the watchers and influencers made us realise how easily programmable the units were. Instil uncertainty and fear and you're halfway there. The rest was cobbled together. It wasn't Scrabble, but we were playing a serious game.

We extended shutdown until what had been presented as a short, sharp, essential shock became the daily norm. As we played it, post-shutdown was taken to be an easing – another level of benefit, frankly, even though the move actually ran from acute and short-term to chronic and permanent. Our Code was revolutionary. "PostShutdown" was how we sold it; time off for all, put your feet up. The suggestion was that for the units to have to speak at all, to use any letters, was a gross imposition. And even if they didn't buy it (though plenty did), they were forced, for the greater good, to, as people used to say, "get with the programme". Considerable time had now to be devoted to what they could say without exhausting their benefit levels, which, as they quickly realised – and as we'd told them would be the case – was a painful condition with chronic symptoms. Naturally, we set our best minds to the task, asking them to come up with a peerless system, the AlphaSyntax.

Our aim here is to guide you through how the benefit developed from the original inspiration, the concept and theory, to the practice, implementation and restructuring of the policy. This we do in order to provide you with a solid foundational understanding. To be clear, the Conversion refers to the entire state. AlphaCode is not an arm, a department, a branch, a focus group, a think-tank. We are not a service, civil or otherwise. We are the state! The Conversion is complete, marking the end of uncertainty and prevarication. Our map of numbers, matrices, models and data, all of which preceded the territorial conversion, indicates a new, improved reality. There will be no backsliding, no return to the status quo. We have leapt through the window of opportunity and taken back control through the total implementation of the AlphaCode. The Conversion is complete.

Those who are assessed fit to use letters receive an allowance that correlates with their condition. Excessive use is monitored through their regular benefit checks at Central House/s and through the watcher patrols (also, increasingly, through the watchers' local report aides). Recovery is the acme of the continuous re-evaluation process that every applicant must undergo; all units are entitled to this if they have demonstrated sufficient effort, assuming that their assessment correlates with this level of need. The local reports bring invaluable data to the table. Recovery is an expensive but ongoing and crucial endpoint to the process. It is also, in the long run, extremely cost-effective. Obviously, the greater the number of units that can be brought to the recovery stage the better. Our research confirms that our method of targeting letter use enables and saves, and we all want that, don't we?

Benefit is calibrated as a monthly allowance (although, in a leisure economy such as ours, the units' sense of time has a tendency to stretch, and payment intervals may stretch too). The leisure economy is another area where we have achieved so much. When we began our work towards the Conversion, concerns were raised about how, once the units were – we hoped – off the streets and out of the picture, society would continue to run. Who would do the dog work, who would fetch, carry and deliver? What about the productivity and growth that are crucial for us to sustain?

While maintaining the reality of the leisure economy for those who deserve such a life, through our minutely tiered system we also reached that perfect moment when it became clear that, in such a technologically advanced society as ours, machines did the work better. Always with an eye on expansion and development (yet more reasons to remove the lazy, unskilled units from the workplace), we recognised that machines work tirelessly, they don't skive, don't cheat. They can even fix malfunctions or breakdowns themselves. This switch to a fully machine-led workplace enabled productivity levels to be upheld during The Hardship and ever since.

Talking of cheating, we have left some elements of the black market – illicit avenues for buying letters – unhindered. Money isn't the only, or even the main, factor about access to letters, but these markets bring their own forms of policing for non-payment, which can lighten our load. (As a side note, money, should you want to buy some, has long since transitioned from metal or paper – dirty/wasteful/resource-depleting materials – and for most people now arrives preloaded onto a microchip, rather than in the form of credit. It can then be used to purchase a small number of essential items.

There are no grounds for complaint. Zero tolerance: no room or appetite for it. No one knows what they're missing, so there's no feeling hard done by, not anymore. Everyone is less the wiser. If you've no outlets and no platform for expression, well, there's no expression. Job done. They're too busy keeping account of what they can say or reporting on those who are not making the most of their benefit. The vast majority of recipients have bought the rhetoric and are keen to ensure that anyone who hasn't also done so is punished accordingly.[49] It's the new neighbourliness. Use it/ lose it becomes a self-fulfilling prophecy as the compliance of the majority leaves the especially Gifted, or those close to

49 A quid pro quo arrangement has proved useful here.

recovery, with even fewer opportunities for speaking. It's true that in a tiny number of extreme cases, benefit levels may be altered for contraventions such as lateness, failure to appear at Central/s, or unspecified non-compliance. This is the best form of education: units come to realise the value of the system and their position in it.

The myriad ways in which we control usage, to ensure the Gifted use only their own allowances, include sanctions,[50] full recovery, and therapeutic sanatoria. There is no "carrying over", no reward for so-called thrift, no market for general use [see: Inestimable Value: Trading and Commodities].[51] There are calibrated penalties for misuse. What is often referred to as "sharing", which is in fact stealing, may be allotted further benefit where appropriate as an incentive.[52] Although it is unethical and somewhat disturbing that people still try to sell their benefits, there's no need for us to take direct action.[53] The final option for the extended care of the Recovered is in the perfectly designed facilities in our peaceful below-ground campus.

Our most effective tool in instilling obedience is the deliberate fostering of uncertainty. If units have letters, they want to keep on having them, especially when they don't know what it will mean to not have them. Fear of the unknown adds a keen edge to the fear of what they are already experiencing. Also, research has shown that social separation and hierarchies develop according to letters (either confirming

50 Much debated, according to anecdotal evidence: everyone is in denial about them, though everyone knows what they are.

51 [**note these are top notes not footnotes**] The idea persisted for some time that a kind of open-access "black market" existed for those with resources to spend on purchasing letters. It is unlikely that this was ever the case, since letters aren't saleable items.

52 The word "reward" is always to be avoided. It sends out the wrong signals.

53 **As mentioned above, for those with access, see *The Kindest Cut: Ultimate Sanction Options.***

or disrupting other petty jealousies, such as money and class, as well as race, creed and colour). Letters serve as a new hierarchy, a new tool of discrimination, weaponised for overall advantage.

The units are happy to get what they're given – it's a more useful distribution of resources, after all. They don't know why they've been assigned different letter allowances. There is no feedback or explanation, no system of appeal. The assumption that they'll get by, sharing, making do, cutting back together to make it possible, often proves not to be the case. This is considered by the policymakers and those who adopted it to be a welcome if not entirely foreseen side effect. It quickly causes ruptures with and within groups, couples, families, friends, siblings, neighbours, and greatly weakens solidarity.[54] Another unforeseen outcome: we didn't think quick wins could be this good. Keeping the units in a state of ignorance has now been incorporated into the system as a happy byproduct and instrumentalised accordingly.

The system is a closed one. Decisions are made according to a set of parameters that are not made publicly available and, in any case, would be far too complex for most people to understand [see: HMRC#24 Negotiating Procedural Parameters]. It's a design of compulsion, for dis-ease, with no respite – on the unit side of the system, that is. Respect? That's not an issue here. Counts for nothing. A mistake, category-wise.

The above text is the official version of
The AlphaConversion – this is a postscript

The system adds up precisely because none of it does, and who's to know? Very few of us, and none of them. That's

54 For those involved in strategy, or even delivery dogs [sorry, trustees], this is probably one of the most valuable "unexpected" gains in terms of weakening social cohesion.

how it works. Or, put another way, very few people know how it *doesn't work*. We say that fear is key, the Code's most powerful instrument of enforcement. We don't say much about how fear works on more than just the units. Almost everyone, it seems, even in the upper echelons of management, is scared stiff of talking too much to anyone outside their immediate circle, of catching anything, of hearing something, of being heard. As long as there are no breaches, who cares what the chatter is like in their little gaggles?

Allocation Specifics

Everyone has their own carefully aggregated, customised benefit of Es and Rs and so on, as many as they need, and regular revision redistributes letters according to use and circumstance. Our research confirms that targeting letter use in this way enables units to function on the barest minimum and saves valuable resources. Can't be faulted, that, now can it? That's what we all want.

Level 1: A E N O R T
Level 2: D G L S U
Level 3: B C F H I M P W X Y
Level 4: J K Q V Z[55]

Note how many of them – and whole runs – are unnecessary for full unitary existence! As benefit levels increase, whole words can be added to their entitlement, to accelerate the advantages and profit. On occasion, when a vocabulary item has been identified as a particular burden, lists of words can enrich the benefit, bringing freedom from the need for repetition.[56]

55 This can be quite fluid according to various regime commissioners. Security level clearance ******.
56 In full consultation with the word-level executive branch via our integrated system.

• No Qs because we deal with questions by providing the answers, relieving units of that burden and all their other burdens. For whom is the letter Q of use, anyway? Even across the foreign mass, is there a country of significance that deems it useful? And no Qs because there's no more lining up. You come when you're called. No waiting and no time wasted.

• No I, because it's all about us and "the Is have it", and sometimes the old ways are best. We're doing it together – this mantra can't be repeated often enough. There's no need for uncertainty and questions – security and trust are in full flow. It's us.

• No ZZZZs because there's no sleeping on the job.

• No Ys will be required since no questions are necessary, as above.

• No Xs – for the many not the few, that is. This cuts unnecessary verbiage, the junk info that nobody needs or wants, like a name in a signature. Because there's no voting anymore, no X marks the spot.[57] It's clear. Everyone knows what they need to know. That's it. It all makes so much sense.

Take away the Cs and Ks, the Js and Gs and at a stroke a terrain of confusion is removed. For units to struggle with these subtle differences is unnecessary. What may be experienced as delicious ambiguity by some is, for non-literati units, a cruel burden, one too great to be universally applicable. Therefore, the removal of Cs, Ks, also Is and Qs, is a bonus applicable to that section of the population whose actions and behaviour warrant it.

It's hard to imagine why any unit would need a W or a V, or why they should have to concern themselves about it. Then

57 X has been retained due to ease of use across all sections of the Gifted, and its multifunctionality; in particular its use in lieu of a "signature".

again, the removal of the F and K was the solution to one of the most insidious engines of protest. So we put a f**king stop to it! Apologies everyone – bad joke. I'm also getting a bit ahead of myself; this is more detail than we need at this stage.

•

Staffing Update: Response to Positives

The switch was made to more technological systems because staff on street duty needed to be cut back, having out-performed expectations.[58] It was ~~another happy accident, or rather~~ a key part of our planning in this regard that success would result in reduced need for policing by our forces. There was much less noise, less bellyaching and less mindless chatter across all classes. It was working well, better than expected – actually, very much better. Moreover, it was self-regulating. Double bubble!

The new tech also meant that another expense was spared: the printing and distribution of allowance booklets that each unit had to "cash in" on a daily basis to obtain the letters they needed for that day. Top-ups were available should there prove to be unexpected talk the day before. It wasn't, of course, possible to recoup letters that had been "cashed" but found to be unnecessary. These rules were implemented to avoid what would have been substantial administrative costs; also to embed the notion of planning – the need for units to know what they had to say beforehand, to calculate usage over the coming week. It was each individual's responsibility to keep abreast of their allocation and their schedule to ensure they would make their provision last. It also kept them busy – quiet and off the streets.

58 Budgetary factors were key here.

•

HMRC#1 Protocol – research paper, in progress

It is said that somehow the literati/alfabi/alfabetti [Comment: full taxonomic descriptions to be inserted] were keen/ had decided/were militating for a global shift to ... not Esperanto but a *lingua uniqa* (singular/solo/universal/single-lingua) among those in benefit. This would be in a special form for their own use. Among the obvious advantages were that those who enjoyed "free" movement would have no difficulty getting their needs met by the staff and fellow units they had to communicate with.[59] A global system of servitude unhindered by regional or national variation would ensue. The demands of switchover would inconvenience them, certainly, but these inconveniences would be short-lived and compensated for by the "ease" that would follow. Assessing benefitee levels would add a secondary but highly useful dimension. Looking towards another future, and acknowledging the possibility (slight, admittedly, though it is) of the unknown, the idea of retaining local languages of diminishing and particularised specialist scope would ensure continued concentration on the job of separation and an absence of irrelevant and diversive conversation. [Comment from editoriat: Commendable language skills. Remarkable precision!]

The burdensome unitary requirement to learn other languages is forthwith lifted. Because we are one, logically it follows that there is no need for more than one language; to have more than one would be divisive (see below).[60] Although those lobbying for them to be retained extolled the benefits of a national

59 This includes any specialist allocation for local dialect, which there is no need to recognise (see below).

60 AlphaCode Conversion does not and will never include other languages; they are beyond our remit and our concern. This has become a bedrock policy, foundational for the maintenance of society's strengths and cohesiveness.

training programme – an argument that has some, albeit small, merit – the high percentage of non-attenders and fails indicated the true direction of travel [see: Welcoming the End of the Esperanto Hoax]. Subjects that incorporated the dangers of worthless – and worse still, soft – knowledge, such as the histories of other cultures, are no longer a risk in terms of depleting resources. As they're no longer an option, they're a non-issue. To say that our own culture is insufficiently rich and unworthy of study would be gross and insulting. We reflect. We speak our own beautiful language with our fellow nationals. That's more than enough. Those who insist on using other languages will, naturally enough, receive maximum support by being fast-tracked for full recovery. We feel their pain. Our thoughts go out to them. Etc. etc.

Also, we intervened and put a stop to other forms of "communication", such as gesture, signage, blinking in code, drawing, kinesics – just a few of the faddish, non-verbal methods that infested and infected the available channels: virtual, ether, soundwaves, walkways, etc. Early fears that legislative powers would need to be invoked were premature. Any form of sign language was likewise deemed beyond the capabilities of large swathes of the population.[61] Anything physical – mime, dance – or audible articulation of a non-verbal kind, such as whistling, wordless singing and humming, were redefined as a public nuisance, as many of us had always considered them to be.

•

Marks on Paper

Punctuation cutbacks immediately post-Hardship were scarcely remarked upon. Most caused no change, barely used

61 But the prospect of fully silenced sections of the population was so appealing that signing was almost taken up. Oh, the quiet!

as they were anyway. The benefit inclusion of the exclamation mark was, it must be confessed, a hard choice, and there was some opposition to it. Ditto the question mark.[62] It had been a good long while since commas, dashes or colons had been used consistently, or indeed at all. Even the full point was rarely seen. Nonetheless, in the early stages, we still had to listen to the moaners and groaners when they tried to speak in a way they thought meaningful of a time when semi-colons divided items on a list, or keyboards had special keys for hyphens and two other types of dash. [Again, check this to ensure correct usage of terminology.] <There was a time ...>, they would begin, or <Back in the day ...>, but everyone knew that what they were talking about was of an earlier time, hence of little concern to all but a few diehard spellers and punctuationists. It was agreed that had the use and misuse of superfluous punctuation continued, action would have to be taken. For a brief period of time, a wave of support for old-style, old-fashioned spelling bees went underground, became an elite sport, and the bees occasionally morphed into acronym or heritage text-speak language quizzes [see: Report on Uprisings/Unsocial Behaviours Leading to Extensions in the Scope of Legislation].

The question of writing was regularly posed in the early major-strategy planning discussions during the early days of the Big Quiet, and in a manner and tone to suggest that all our hard work would amount to nothing. Presumably the thinking behind this – apart from an unfathomable and apparently fathomless desire among some of our so-called supporters to find fault and undermine the success of the system – is that writing allows covert letter use. Because it can be seen but not heard, it's all but impossible to monitor and oversee. However, given that it necessitates the use of

62 Questions and questioning are not pursuits for the Gifted; see above on Q and Y in particular. Consistency is what the units need, as is their right, and to deliver it is part of the AlphaCode remit.

materials that, for the most part, are no longer available, this is irrelevant. Paper is highly prized, an increasingly rare commodity, and its purchase, along with pens and pencils, requires a special permit. Because the application process to receive a permit is stringently controlled, those who will probably not manage paper well are, for their own safety, disbarred.[63]

Considerable time has elapsed since writing was a skill deemed necessary to lead a full and meaningful life. But in truth it's an encumbrance, weighing down everybody with the same requirements, with no thought given to use or talent. In the equitable society with which we are now blessed, full account is taken of criteria such as ability, capacity and need. In the few schools that remain [see: The Dark Educator Nexus] there's a special pathway by which those needing to write may contribute to some historical or archival endeavour.[64] Otherwise this activity is largely irrelevant and should not be allowed to continue to drain resources.

A new industry was developed for self-inking stamps that provided predictive (and predictable) phrases for use in everyday situations, such as "Hello", "Rotten weather, isn't it?", "I suppose so", and "Goodbye". For many units, a handful of stamped phrases were all they needed: simple, fast, reusable, and blessedly limited in scope.

The AlphaCode communication systems with ~~recips~~[65] units is second to none. Messages and results arrived by red feather, as noted – a nod to times past and outmoded com-

63 This includes those whose intended usage is considered suspect.

64 The project to reduce such "endeavours" is underway, though regrettably it remains at an early stage.

65 This term, which circulated persistently in some office environments, was banned early on in the programme due to its misleading and derogatory implications.

munication formats. Sometimes, in the early days, the red feather was "real", an actual red feather delivered secretly in person by watchers, but mostly it was a projection or image, usually positioned for general viewing by units at Central House/s and delivered secretly by watchers. It was realised early on that message-by-feather did not need to be as technologically advanced (and expensive) as an activatable chip. Some kind of physical "reminder" (or shock) would do just as well. Really, what had been implanted is fear and, by way of that, compliance. In the early days, when tech still had an almost global reach, that's how messages arrived. Eventually, for policy reasons, verbal or written reminders were abandoned. Officially, this was on grounds of sustainability – saving paper, etc. The majority, once their red feather had arrived, heaved a sigh of relief. It signaled their temporary release from the anxiety of having to deal with letterwork, from worry about saying the wrong thing or saying too much. Fearing the arrival of the next tranche of letters, post-red feather, also proved useful in enforcing compliance. Fewer letters = less chat and less chat = less anxiety.

•

Masking

Warning! Some readers, trustees in particular, may find the following material upsetting, but there's simply no avoiding it. We need to talk about mask usage.

It is a truism that the Gifted, as well as being unskilled in communication, are unskilled in other ways. Staying healthy, for example, which is predicated on basic hygiene. To avoid the possibility of coming into contact with their bodily fluids or vapours, us Coders must always wear a mask.

The scale of the protective coverings we've made available

varies according to single unit or group and the level of danger commensurate with the expected or suspected level of contact. We aim to make the full mask range available in all Central House/s to accommodate every member of the workforce, whatever their level. This will include protective gear for nose and mouth, full face, upper body, and even, in the most extreme circumstances, total coverage (footwear included). Also, the barrier between staff and others, maintained by the greeter and signposter, must not be breached.

Once upon a time we masked up merely as a precaution, to hide our identities. But the protective element has become increasingly important as the threat to health has increased. What was once merely a life-changing circumstance is now life-threatening. Even when fully protected, we must all keep to the prescribed areas: pathways, processes and forms of meeting and expression. To do otherwise is reckless and dangerous. Criminal, too [see under Mask Abuse in the penal code]. If you wish to maintain your status as a trustee, a provider, and indeed a recipient of this special and generous system, you must comply with the masking rules. That goes doubly so for the units, needless to say. End of story.

•

Down to Details: Names and Numbers

The anonymity conferred by the wearing of masks is only one part of our programme, which works across digital and physical encounters. These are not in-person encounters as such. They are with units who must be assessed and given the help they need so that they may reap the benefits that accrue from our system.

Although we all use the same processes, the same methods,

the same words to communicate, the units' difficulties with naming were all-too-painfully apparent. It was our duty to reduce those difficulties, not add to them. Accordingly, whatever names they once may have used are now of no concern. That's past. They are to be identified only by their individual letter entitlement. Names are no longer needed and no longer used, and what a blessing that is for all concerned.

A numbering system was implemented for a while, followed by codes. But in terms of generation and maintenance they were equally wasteful and long since abandoned. Bear in mind that anything that could be perceived as offering a "personalised service" in relation to issues other than benefit levels is a contravention of procedure. The letter status of each unit is all that matters. On the few occasions when onscreen engagement is deemed necessary, randomly supplied images of faces are available for staff use. Anonymity is all. Interactions that suggest a "personal touch" are to be avoided. As are repeated one-to-one sessions. These are dangerous in that they can easily lead to a breach of the protocols of service, resulting in an over-generous application of benefit and a contravention of the code. Such gross misconduct will not be excused, and perpetrators will receive no second chance. Punishment will be meted out for any delay to the curative process. The entitled must not, no matter what, have their progress towards full recovery disrupted for any reason whatsoever. The letter status of each unit is all that matters.

5. Resistance Mechanisms

Here are the words of the Wall-Es, a kind of underground army, a resistance group on our side. For readers who have not come across Wall-Es in person or by hearsay, let me explain: they were an independently organised, self-denying, self-sacrificing force working to save people from the effects of the Alphabet Tax. The Wall-Es tried to make a difference, they tried – sometimes at terrible personal cost – to make us speak, to show us that there could be another, brighter future. It can seem as though we all rolled over and accepted whatever the Taxers said without quibble, enabling them to do what they did. The Wall-Es prove that wasn't the case.

They didn't take The ATax lying down. They resisted. They stood against the Code, insisted that it really was a tax. They came together against the authorities and their pronouncements and procedures. They said: "The letters are ours by right, all of them, and the Taxers mustn't be allowed to take them away from us." "Let's talk" – that was their founding statement. From the very beginning they saw the so-called "benefit" as a dictatorial imposition from those at the very top. They refused ever to call it that. Cuts, they called it. Tax. To the very end the Wall-Es saw the Code as a violation of fundamental human rights.

They worked undercover, behind the wall, beneath the radar, tirelessly. They wanted everyone, all the people, to have the same letters, every single one: the full 26. "It's up to us," they said, "not them. They want complete control. They want to make us be quiet. Despite what they say, there is no benefit! They are stealing the letters from us. They want to force us underground, into the tunnels, to keep us quiet. They are taxing our alphabet, stealing our speech, silencing those of us without power or money to stand against them. They want us to have nothing to say and nothing to say it with. They're taking our letters away and giving nothing in return."

At any place or time, suddenly they'd appear, usually in pairs, and start a conversation, casual like. "If we keep talking," they'd say, "the ATaxers can't stop us, whatever they might say to the contrary. They can't hear you, you know. They don't know what you're saying or how often you say it or how many letters it takes. The Alphabet Tax is nothing but a scam; they're scammers." The Wall-Es would mention extra letters and repeats and sharing. They'd get you to sing and practise talking. Sadly, there wasn't much else they could do, and there were plenty of good reasons to run a mile rather than listen to their dangerous talk. But the risks the Wall-Es were taking were greater still, and they had other problems to contend with, such as spies.

To say that the Wall-Es were just a few malcontents, little more than a minor irritant to the Taxer project, is greatly to undervalue their contribution to our struggle. I mean, no one really knows how many of them there were originally and how few survived the tunnels. The survivors often don't want to talk about their experiences. That's understandable. Still feels dangerous to stir up such bad memories; a threat to their mental health. Many of them were caught while going about their subversive work, mostly outed by Code infiltrators, of which there were many. Here we've included transcripts from Central House of undercover operatives, discussing their infiltration of the Wall-E cells. We hope that through giving space to such voices, creating space for all voices, in time the extent and value of the Wall-Es' work will become clearer.

"You saw one of them Wall-Es?
Never met one, ever. Didn't believe you existed. Can't be real.
Was like you woke us up again, making us talk.
You one of them full-handers n'all? Didn't believe that was true neither."

The passage above is an extract from a Wall-E's testimony, given to the archive with a message: "This conversation gave me the will to keep going as a resistance operative, knowing that we had to help in some way." Let me remind you, a "full-hander" is someone who still has access to all 26 letters of the alphabet. From the tone of this exchange, it sounds likely that the speaker is a three-hander or even a two-hander, with an allocation of only 15 or 10 letters respectively.

•

GD, Respondent to Wall-E Archive Section Questionnaire

You never know who they are, the Wall-Es. You might be one for all I know. I might be one. You don't know, nor do I. You just don't. When they turn up it's a surprise because they look just like us, and that's because they are us! That's what they tell us, anyway. What it is, the difference, is that they don't want benefit, none of it, nothing, not even what they can lay their hands on easy. And they want the rest of us to do without it, too. They want to give the letters back to us. "Take back what's ours." "Take back control." "#Utoo" – all over the place. They keep on and on. "#WTF," more like. Sorry, can't help it: just old-skool, me. And they want everyone else to keep what they have; want us all to do the same. They say it'll bring an end to the Taxer regime. Maybe so. But then what?

They say we owe it to ourselves and to our children to make sure this dangerous Central House Alphabet Tax nonsense is stopped. It's like bible stuff for them – you had that? Hope? They keep saying it. We don't want shutdown, they say; we want to open up, to listen to everyone. They want us to know how much the Code costs us, too. They say it's not how we're told. It's not a benefit. The other thing – what's it called again? They know the name. Can't say that one no more, me. They say we have a party and we all move, like with noise and make letter noise. Back learny-day again, they say, whatever that is. But for our good this time. That's what they say. They say a lot of things and they do look like us. Almost. Bit different, though. The way they carry themselves. And because of using all the letters they don't really sound like us. Funny business, is it? Not sure. Only a short party, then we carry on and they go. The 26 they call it. How many don't know it. 26? I dunno. Can't be that many, surely. Where the Wall-Es go afterwards, no one sees. They go quietly, mysteriously. Unseen. We'll get it all back, they say, give up benefit. Ha-Ha-Ha-ing, is it? If only we really could have it all back, I say.

•

Anon – archive records

I was talking to someone, can't say the name, one of those wall people. Wall-Es, we call them. Or is it Wallys? We call them that because it's like they've gone through the wall, or come through it. Are they stupid or what, putting up a fight? They're there and then they're not. They're like us but not us. How to know who you can talk to, what you can say? If they're here, among us, then I suppose they're the same as us. It used to be harder to know, to tell if they were really Taxer spies come down to hear what we were saying, to check it wasn't wrong. Them watchers and the others: creeps. Always trouble. And some people got taken away for special training. When they don't come back to us afterwards, we wonder: Too special now, are they? Gone somewhere else, up there in Central. Given a job. A long time since any of us has had one of those. Maybe they really are better than us. Anyway, we never hear from them again. It's a secret, too good to share with us. My friend's brother, he goes and we never hear from him again. He was always wanting other letters, more of them, always trying to find new ways to get them. But it's not a market. That's right: market, old style. We're not buying and selling, we get them given. Leisure economy, they cuckoo. You hear from others that you can do it different. Go to buy? With what? – that's what I want to know. Maybe it's not even true. That's not what it's supposed to be like. You get in big trouble and then there's the extra training. And then what? The tunnels, that's what.

People, lots of them, go quiet after a while. Every time the Coders bring in a new force or add some kit, more cameras, more watchers, it makes for more quiet. Big Quiet, even – yeah, right – they fell for it. It's too hard to keep thinking of new ways to use what you've got left, and there's less and less that can be said. Too hard to keep struggling to make less and less be enough. Like a dimmer. An off-button. Stuck on mute. And if you don't use it, you lose it. And then they say <Oh, this is obviously too much of a weight on your shoulders to have so many letters to deal with. We'll take this terrible burden from you.> I haven't heard yet of anyone being made total Delite. Burden-free, they'd say. Completely Gifted – that's what they call complete recovery. Deathly, like. It's big trouble if they hear you say delite or tax. And no one I know can manage the whole a-bet anymore.

•

Compliance Interview Transcript: RT, Wall-E

I'm a Wall-E. Yes, I freely admit it. They used to call us that because it was like we'd come out of the wall, appeared from nowhere, then returned forthwith whence we came. We try to get people to remember, to talk, to share letters. Like underground alphactivists. But it doesn't always happen. Some people – ouch! OK then, I'll call them units if I must – don't believe who we are, think we're trying to trick them and report them and they'll get shunted off down the tunnels. We know it's true about the tunnels. That's where the Recovered go, and all the others you Taxer shits want rid of. Ouch! Gets pretty quiet down the tunnels, I can tell you.

New systems get drawn up all the time by our various cells, but they always get banned outright once you Taxer lot – ouch! – get a sniff. Sometimes the systems are so secret hardly anyone gets to know about them. Anything like signs or symbols are outlawed for being recognisable. Or they're banned because of "dangers of over-sharing". Or they're counted as talking in other languages, and that's not allowed either. And when they're not recognisable as letters – some made-up gesture system – it's so local it never catches on, never really works. We call it FnFs, like the old "Friends and Family", those few you can still talk to in secret. Please, can I stop now. Is that enough?

•

Testimony: JB, Wall-E

They have to keep practising. We keep telling them that. Keep doing it, don't lose it – have to find new ways of saying it, over and over. What's more important, really? That's us, the voice of the cynic, the politically engaged. A lack of practice brings its own rewards for the Taxers – doing their work for them – and they know that, that's the idea. So that makes it even worse. Can't afford to lose more, not now.

Nothing is more important than that. Gotta keep doing it. That's what gets us going in the first place. It takes us a long time to get going because of our fears of being discovered, of being cheated and fooled. Even scared that what we're thinking is just mad nonsense that doesn't make any sense and won't help anyone. And what would we do, exactly, even if we managed to find a fellow thinker or two? Form a cell? Lots of different ideas about what's needed and how we'd do it. Hard enough to get us together at any time. If one of our lot don't show up, you're never sure whether something's happened to them. Maybe nothing. Maybe just an unscheduled Central visit. Or maybe gone for good. Then you wouldn't know whether to mourn them or cuss them out for being a scab. Awful when it's one of your own, but it can turn out like that. Them you'd best forget.

All sorts of people come to the bank, for all sorts of reasons. That sounds like a politician's answer, doesn't it? You'd be surprised. We certainly are. Because of so many ideas about how to reverse the tax, we try lots of different ways to get to people. Calling it a bank and calling us Wall-Es stuck, two of the more lasting names. It's really risky, the letterbank. We were thinking about the old days, those voucher things after the time of The Hardship. History stuff, that. Before they could track letter usage with the cameras and whatnot, no record of leftover letters, what wasn't used. Before the watchers, that was. Before the grasses. Then you couldn't say a word. Not safe to say anything unplanned. Completely against everything the ABTax stands for, the Wall-Es' letterbank thing. Against the law? Well, it's not really like that anymore. If you don't need no benefit and you have money, then you get to decide what's law and what isn't. Everything's about money, so if you're paying you're allowed. Brainwash, we say: it's only money. No letters or only the ones they say, then you've got nothing, no right to say anything. You couldn't say anything – and that's the whole point. The only decision you get to make is to comply, to do what they say.

It isn't ever the law that you can't write anything. Nothing like when people used to vote in parliwotsit. Government is cut away, way before my time. There's like a show – an exhibition maybe they call it. Empty nonsense, that's government now. So, no laws exactly, no governing rules we know about, only about letters and that. But rule is imposed, that's for sure.

•

Report 00Underop1

Even though I've been undercover with the Wall-Es for some years now, I tell you, it's hard to get your head around what they say. Makes no sense but I keep trying.

For a start, it's always "the people", never units. Us Coders, we know that the Tax, as they call it, has been devised to help "people". Sorry, boss, their words not mine, I know it's offensive. You want to get them strung up for that, if nothing else. Benefit revisions – more benefit, right, meaning fewer letters? But according to the WEs it's not a benefit at all, it's punishment. They're backwards about everything. Look at it the wrong way, deliberately so in my opinion. It's not taking anything away, it's giving! That's what we're all about: giving to the units, those most in need. But the WEs just don't get it that the units don't have any use for extra letters, and that increasing their benefit to reduce their letters will make their lives easier and better. More cost effective too. After all this time, after all the obvious social improvements the Code has brought about, the WEs still won't have it. That hasn't changed during all my time pretending to be one of them. I've never met one who'd budge an inch. It's a scandal. They're all as guilty as hell. They go on and on about their duty and those precious days when friends and family could still chat to each other. On and on they go – all documented in the full report.

The WEs don't even understand that this quiet is how we want it. Units get what they deserve and not a letter more. That's the plan and it's working. Quiet! One Wall-E I bring in for re-education keeps wailing <How did it happen? How did we let it happen? Why did we?> He also said that none of the units need the Code contract, but everyone gets it.

Units can feel it, see it, taste it. If we say it often enough it becomes true. That's the reality of it, he said. Units just take it, sit there, scared, bored witless. Finished. And not far off speechless, soon enough. The WEs wish it weren't so. Win-win, then, for us.

Red feathering was, let's be clear, an on-the-spot treatment provision. And believe me, nothing was ever in-your-face enough to make it clear to some of the units that they were hereby, from that moment on, relieved of any further letter-work. Luckily, they fell for it. We put one out for an after-noon or a couple of hours whenever we felt like it, for all of them coming that day to Central House/s. They really were stupid enough to believe it was there just for them! Like they were special or something.

•

Testimony: DM, Wall-E

Even before "We Hear You", all soft and friendly, turned into "We Hear YOU", with massive black letters reaching across whatever space it was plastered on, solid and square, some people were starting to get the picture. "This isn't right, we have to do some-thing, this is going too far, what can we do?" That's what those of us who went on to become Wall-Es asked ourselves. We had no idea then how far it would go.

Like everyone, we'd seen the "We Hear You" signs all over the place, but it was a big shock when they changed. How they did it so fast and we never saw it happening we'll never know. But the pale blues and yellows and pinks turned jet black overnight. "We Hear YOU" was a frozen warning after the warm(ish) glow of its predecessor. We didn't know exactly what the warning was about ... not then, not yet. Early days, as I say. But there was no misun-derstanding what it meant: do this, don't do that, or else.

•

Getting together isn't supposed to happen. Can't talk, so what's the point? It happens anyway. Getting together to swap letters, give letters, share letters, even talk about letters – if you do that you're going to be down the hatch right away. I reckon every one of us Wall-Es has different ideas about what we ought to do. We believe different things too. Some of us think it isn't true about the tunnels and the disappeared. Some think the whole distribution system is a nonsense – how would the ACoders know if everyone kept on using the full hand, all 26? Unless, that is, they're told – and I don't mean by monitors or chips, I mean by people who count it up for them. But there aren't enough snitchers and watchers for them to do it properly. No way. Even so, some of them believe all of it, still. For them, being a Wall-E is a way of giving free help to those most in need. I know, I start off believing in it, but it isn't long before I stop. What an idiot, even if it don't take me long!

I wanted to do the Wall-E thing, to help people who can't help themselves. Charidee some call it. We want to be Wall-Es to help our most vulnerable, so they say. Or maybe they're the Coder types telling it false. I'm not sure. Either way. You only meet a few of the people. Small cells only. No communication between them. For reasons of safety, so that if one of ours turns out to be one of them, a plant, a weasel, they can only finger a few of us, not the whole lot, none of the other cells.

How it happens, how you get through the barrier of incomprehension, the wall, is you say something like: "I've changed my mind, don't think this Alphabet Tax is a good idea any more, far from it." Someone hears. Ears and eyes everywhere, ours and theirs.

DA, Wall-E – session transcript (from memory)

"OK, tell me what you've got, then. Anything useful? We can do a deal, pay you a little something. C'mon, tell me and I'll meet you later and …"

"You'll give me meat?"

"Oh, funny boy aintcha. C'mon, get real! I'll give you something for them though. We're short on Rs and Ws. Can manage without one but not both. Or Cs, we'll pay you for them too."

"Two sees? What's that for?"

"Ah, got it. You can do the talking but no writing, is that it?"

"Long gone, mate. I once had a screen thingy, with keys. And pens. And words on paper. But now … nah, forgot it all."

"Yeah, okay, let's get on with it then. It's like a bank. You remember? For spend spend stuff, or food – free. You need, we give; then you have. Or for an hour or a whole day – that's a borrow. If it helps, we work out what you need most. We're staying here, can come again, for others."

"A hole day? Is that for sleep time?"

•

Testimony: WP, Wall-E

We tried letter fasting, to share what we had. At that stage the level of self-denial, self-silencing, became quite extreme. Many of them experienced dizziness and fainting spells. Some had to give up and start using again; great disappointment for them, particularly because no one had come up with any other way of stockpiling letters. The pile in stockpile is something of an exaggeration. It's a small store and it runs down to nothing quicker than you can say – ach, you know. There are some, only a few, who want it all or nothing, don't appreciate what they're offered. Throw it back sometimes. After such a famine you can understand it, I suppose. Most are hungry for whatever they can get after The Hardship, the shut-downs, the quiets, on and on. Can't see that even a little more would help, even if not making much of a difference yet.

You learn to swallow your words, to save the letters. Takes a lot of trial and error, that, coughing them out again in the right way so we can keep them. Early on you get away with some storing, keeping some back every time. Slow progress, though. When the Tax ramps up, they bring in the "use by" system, and it takes a bloody long while to work around it.

We aren't local, that wouldn't be safe. Each cell of Wall-Es moves round to the next place, a different one each time. Every visit a different place, unfamiliar. But even though we don't get to know each other and don't meet, we find ways to leave notes, pass on ideas. What works, what doesn't, what we haven't got around to or time to try. The Tax is completely centralised, but even those people are human, just about, so there's always room for error, hence local variations. And we can't assume that all Taxers are "sick animals of evil intent," as one of my Wall-E cellmates put it. OK, well, you know what I mean.

Remember accents? Someone worked out this whole system of how letters sound different, like other letters in different places. Worked a bit; haphazard, though. Then there's speaking reeeeaal-llllly slooooooowly. Looks like it takes more letters, I know, but only when you see it like this. Then there's speaking vvvfast, whispering or shouting. Again, in the early days, you could get away with a lot. Worth a try. But the fear stems all that after a while.

•

Report 00 UnderOp2

I never know how many of them there are. I know our group, five in the end, and I think one of our lot is part of another

Wall-E three. But I could be wrong and it could be more. Not much talking goes on about it. I'm not joking, they're incredibly tight-lipped! Annoyingly so. No chat, no <they do it differently in this or that group>. Nothing to report on.

Once they do get to talking, they start to realise we can't know everything, or even very much. We can't know whether the letters they're using are spent or not. Some of the Wall-Es, if not the units, have clocked that the recording devices don't do any recording, and then realise what that means about how the trustees know who's said what: hearsay and grassing people up. But do they know that's true about the recorders and stuff? They think it's an act. The trouble for the WEs is that it's an act everyone believes in. Or if they say they don't, they're in big trouble and they'll soon be disappeared. That's what happens. They don't know for sure, but they do get that anything coming out of Centrals, the whole thing, supposedly based on the science, data-driven, minutely engineered and whatnot, is not what it seems.

It has to be for free, they nearly all agree on that, no returns. For nothing. No exchange – really, nothing. Not everyone believes that's right. It takes a long time, back and forth between the five of us, then the passing to the other group, the three, and then on from them, probably by way of notes left in strategic places. I never found out how it works, not really, but it has to go right across everyone who says they want to be part of it. On basic stuff they all have to agree to do the same, even if they don't always like it. Big arguments about that. It's the first discussion they have, even before deciding what exactly it is they're going to do. That's maybe why it takes so long to reach an agreement. Two of our lot want there to be payment in kind, some sort of exchange. <Why should they get this for free when it's us who are doing all this work to make it available and taking the biggest risks?> That's what they think. Could be a sign for us of the extent of our reach – that the Conversion really is taking hold.

<It's a massive thing we're giving them, so they should respect that by giving something back.> That's how they think about it. Some of them anyway. But it's so much part of what they want to leave behind. Part of the difficulty is that they don't know what anyone has left to offer in return. That's another avenue us Coders have successfully blocked. To galvanise and unite the vast majority of the units against the WEs – now that's definitely a mark of our success! Another one. Units unite: good, eh?

•

Testimony: CK, Wall-E

Did I mention the talk about the letters being free? I'm not so sure about this one. Like, if it's true, how did the Code ever happen? But it's just as bad if it's not true. For the Delites, it's a bit much to expect them to get that. We're all Delites, really; only a few of us Wall-Es still holding out. None of them want to know where the extras come from; the letters, I mean. No one asks. But they all ask where we come from, how did we get there. And where precisely is "there"? Places where we know we'll find people. Or, later on, we ask them to come to where we are, people who'll be interested.

To do it you have each to take a vow of silence, otherwise you have no chance of collecting enough letters. That's a big laugh right there, and lots of people won't do it, think we're some of those Taxer shits. Can't blame them really. Being silent to end the silence: no wonder they think we're them. And we appear from nowhere, like the red feather, but instead of insisting that people clam up, we're asking them to talk. And although they call it an exchange, it's not about lending and borrowing, we're giving.

That's how it is. Then we get down to talking about what it is we're giving, how we can offer them letters. That's the real stuff. How to do it best takes another load of talk, a lot of convincing. Planning the conversations – that's a minefield. When and where and how to get it done without making it obvious what we're doing. We don't have much else to do, so having this to pour time into isn't a bad thing, not for us. Like having a special assignment, but not like the kind of job where you turned up at the same time and place every day. Remember that?

You'll have to ask the others what they get out of doing the Wall-E stuff. I'd say it's the giving, trying to change it back to what it was like without the benefit. So not really like a bank at all. How it was before all that tax shit. You could call it safekeeping, in a way, but really the point of it isn't to keep anything, it's to give it away, freely. That's right. We don't even know what we're aiming for, exactly how many letters we want to save or why we need them.

•

SB, Wall-E in Conversation with Alfab – transcription excerpt

"You think it's fixed forever like this?
        [silence]
"What I'm saying now, it's about the words, taxing you, taxing your tongue.
        [silence]
"Words. What they're made of. Letters. Small data. Bits. Build them up to talk. Remember that?
        [small sigh, perhaps regretful]
"Can you think back to before tax?
        [silence]
"How are you fixed, come to that?
        [silence]
"Only one way for that to go. You went learny-day ever?
        [silence]

"Alfbt now. A-l-p-h-a-b-e-t. Used to call it that. At learny-day. Ah, yes. P. H. But you still got T?

     [Alfab shakes head]

"Oh. B, yes? Mmm. Good one, that. Five-hands of them, that's the full hand — well, give or take. You a three-hander?

     [Alfab holds up both hands]

"Two, ah."

•

RR, Wall-E – dream testimony

"Eat after reading" the letters said. It was a dream, but I thought I'd won. The letters hurt the hand. Cold, burning cold. So then I don't want to use that letter again, won't say it. And it disappears in front of my face. Can't use liquid for letters, can I? That was the start. Freeze or burn them into existence. And this voice telling me <Use the basic elements in a transformed state.> Eh? <Make that miraculous shift into otherness of form through tempera-ture and dimension.> Whaaat? Another Wall-E said something like that and that's why it came back to me in my sleep. Beyond me, even in a dream.

Letters like ice cubes. They melt away while I watch, before I can put them in the order I want. The letters disappear, the sense dissolves. The quicker you try to use them the warmer they get and the sooner they liquify. You destroy the letters through use. Because handling melts them, you use them less, and the less you use them the fewer you have. Here we go again: consumption or abstention: the choice isn't yours. Just a dream, though, nothing to worry about. Or you destroy them by watching and waiting. Even looking and breathing on them can do it. If you're quick, and if it's cold enough, you can use them before they disappear. Hurts like they're hot even when it's cold. Scorching, in fact.

Not a dream, just another nightmare. Woke up crying. When I

woke up again, proper awake, I knew what I had to do – go join the Wall-Es.

•

On one level, the Wall-Es want everyone to join them, but they also know they have to keep it small. Too risky otherwise. And they're aware of the dangers of entryism or infiltration, know it can be a problem. Can't be denied, even if it is more of a suspicion. There's very little info about it. But boy, are they suspicious.

A bigger problem is the Gifted not trusting them. Not surprising, that, but at the time they couldn't believe how strongly some units reacted against them. It's annoying for them, upsetting. Like it's them stealing or taking something from the units. <Where did you get those letters, anyway?> – that's what they mean. So the units are doing our policing for us. Gotta laugh. That's another big result. The units aren't trusting that WE-giving nonsense; they know that getting the extras from the Wall-Es isn't like getting more benefit. One time I see one of the WEs cry – yes, really – when this other unit hasn't a clue what to do with the extra letters. That was quite a while back, too. In a few places they try setting it up so that anyone can donate, but it's too much to organise for most, they can't keep it going, and by all accounts they lose sight of what it is they're trying to do: bank letters for free distribution to alfabs.

Yeah, alfabs. You not heard that one before? Some of the units come up with it to avoid using the same old terms – delites, gifted, all that. It's funny when you think about it, it isn't our language they use but it's all about us. They couldn't talk like us if they tried, even if they had all 26. Not ever.

The Wall-Es are upset that the units don't respond more positively. They expect them to get angry about their situation. Here's a recording of one of them moaning on:

> "Over the months and years you can hear people struggling because they can't manage on what they've got. They're getting less and less, most of them, nearly all of them, and they're managing less well too. The worst of it is they think it's their own fault. They don't seem to realise it's through no fault of their own, unless you count capitulation as a fault, giving in, giving up. What they don't get is how it came to be like this. People believe the rubbish they're told at Central House. It's like they believe that if they're being treated in this way, like it doesn't matter what they say, it's because they don't count. Maybe it's not what they're told, it's how they're treated – no respect, no politeness, no explanations. Basically, no understanding that they're human and don't deserve to be treated in such a demeaning way. I'd say they treat you like you're an animal, but it's a long time since there was a difference that made any difference, know what I mean? After all, we *are* animals.

> "Some question – among ourselves, anyway – why it's them getting less and less and not him down the road. Others have the same amount as years gone by; people keep hold of three, four hands-worth of letters still. Can't work out why. Still can't. No way of finding out. No one to ask. Not that you'll get a proper answer from anyone, anyway."

This kind of talk lifts the spirits – how far the Conversion

has come. Our work on the Code has taken hold, powerfully.
<My own fault.> That's what they end up saying, one way or
another. <All down to me.> As if they had anything to do
with it.

•

Testimony: JH, Wall-E

They say they're going to grant me the use of letters, and for a
while I believe they really mean that. You know, all of them, the
full set. How many was it again – 25, 26? Was I happy to hear that?
Of course. But surely it can't be true. They talk and talk. I remember feeling bewildered because it went on so long. Then I felt
drowsy, so I'm not even sure I was able to follow what was being
said. I suppose you'd call it a browbeating. I remember thinking:
They're talking me into submission, or at least talking me to sleep.
Yes, I suppose they may have given me something – put it in the
water – but I don't know what and I don't know if I actually did
fall asleep. I don't even remember whether I drank the water.
Where I've been you don't drink the water, it's just not safe.

Granting me access. It's free, like a gift. Or maybe they say "gifting"
– I think that's what they say. Don't recall. It's special, not for
everyone, they say. For me, they say. They also say something
about letters on paper. Writing letters to send, like no one else
knows what that is, and I say, "Mmm, yes, press send, I done that",
so they know I'm worth receiving what they want to give me.
Maybe a job? Years since I've done one of those. Maybe they know
that; trying to catch me out. I clock them sharing a glance when I
say that, like "She's got it, she can have them." Then the spell is
broken, I don't know how. Don't know how they do it in the first
place: make people believe they're right and we have to do what
they say even though we don't like it one little bit.

But some people are so far gone they want the Code back; out of stupefaction. They've totally lost it, don't know what to do with themselves. We Wall-Es are lucky – they used to call us lucky, those of us who came through unscathed. There are plenty who got caught out, though, and ended up down the hatch. Never will know how many. We think we'll find more of them somewhere. Survivors. Not seen any so far.

I can't bear to think they're that clever, that they could have known or even imagined how the bits of their ramshackle system – the quiets, the watchers, the hearers, the assessments, the cameras, the recorders, and all the rest – would fit together and actually work to stop everyone talking. Gotta keep thinking that they've just been lucky, given that it most likely wasn't foreseen by them, that they weren't smart enough to plan this. But it worked and they didn't have to lift a finger to keep it working. Lucky, is it? I'd say so. Until their luck ran out.

6. Application and Entitlement

Again, a warning from the archivists: What follows is unsettling and may, for some readers, be deeply upsetting. Please proceed with caution.

While you've been reading through the sections of this report – more of which may enter the archive as we uncover further documents, and more still may be created through our open forums – you can't have failed to notice that the expressions in the Coders' documents become, as time goes by, more insulting and frighteningly aggressive. Between themselves, the largely anonymous authors obviously felt no need to sugar the pill. It's clear they knew exactly what they wanted to achieve, if not always how to go about it. How they got where they wanted to be is exposed in hapless, chaotic fashion through multiple versions of their writings and recordings, all of which reveal their mismanagement and incompetence. Despite having no actual way of assessing benefit levels, or anything else for that matter, they still got what they wanted. People used to say, "Don't believe everything you read in the newspapers", and mostly we didn't, not that we had newspapers by then. Turns out we wouldn't have been able to tell the difference, anyway.

Those diktats and homilies, the speeches, manifestos and treatises, agendas and declarations – on and on and on – speak volumes about the scheme the ATaxers imposed on us. What's especially notable is their wilful disregard of the devastation it caused – indeed, set out to cause. Total cynicism. The records, in all their itemised filth, will be retained because there's a genuine need to know. That's the plan, for now at least.

The Taxers may be gone, but their words and deeds can never be erased from our minds, our psyches, and even, as seen earlier, from our buildings. We should never forget that this happened to us, and because it happened once it could easily happen again. No one should feel obliged to read our report, but everyone has to know it's there, available for consultation.

These excerpts from the standard script for trustee use in training and interpretation give real-time insight into the bread-and-butter issues involved in maintaining the system.

> <Answer yes or no, that's all that's needed. Those are the options. And yes is the right answer.>

This makes the process quicker and easier for all concerned, especially for those in most need. It is designed to add benefit to those already enjoying receipt.

> < Your next appointment will be at this time, unless or until you are told otherwise. You must arrive 10 minutes early on each occasion.[66] If you fail to do so, your benefit level will be reassessed.>

There is no deviation, no "special circumstance", no dispensation, no individual. Just a plan and a script for trustees to follow to ensure absolute equality of application, the highest possible achievement.

> <Yes or no?>

The following exchanges between AlphaCode officers and a member of the Gifted community were recorded for use in learning situations with new trustees. In the first circumstance, the AlphaCoders were alerted to a possible misdemeanour by exterior enforcers who found the unit *in flagrante* – talking distractedly, with no self-restraint whatsoever. Because the unit was watching neither its mouth nor its letters, it was taken to the special implementation-of-care suite to assess and address its level of responsibility, the extent and nature of the offence and the verdict as to what should be done.[67]

---

66 This is an early hurdle that many fail to cross. If they do not arrive punctually, as requested, ten minutes before the appointed time, they are deemed late and in breach. The usual sanction for failure in relation to punctuality is immediate and total cancellation. Lengthened wait time, which could be seen as a reward, is not recommended as an alternative.

67 Via Tracey profiling (for an explanation, see p43).

Through a process of exchange and upskilling, the outcome for the unit turned out to be positive, it proved capable of being transformed. That should always be the preferred AlphaCode route.

You say what?

<This is the right thing to do. That is our priority.>

Get up, out the door.

<In this way, your forward motion is secured.>

Show me.

<A positive outcome is assured.>

This is not a ...

<At all times the positive is underscored. AlphaCode can only be the right thing.>

This is not ...

<No time is wasted on peripherals.>

Business as usual.

Business as usual.

<Units are required to attend all sessions. Absence will not be tolerated.>

That Central. Go there, now!

< No exceptions. No exclusions are possible.>

Not just me then, is it?

<A suitable trial period will lead to immediate improvement and the extension to benefit can then be ratified.>

You say?

What follows is evidence of the AlphaCode's charitable approach and sensitive nature, as well as its efficacy. It should be noted that the unit involved in these exchanges is now in complete recovery. Quite the result, I think you'll agree!

Roleplay for Trustees

<Admit it. Say it. Say it!>

I wrote ... I wrote a letter to ...

<I? I? You wrote a letter? You? A letter?>

I wrote ...

<Press here for yes. Now!>

[Groan]

<You wrote a letter. To whom did you write this letter?>

A letter ...

[Silence]

<Who to? To whom did you write the letter?>

To my love. I wrote a letter to my love and ...

<Now, tell us which letter. Which letter did you write? Which one? Was it one of yours? Was it one of theirs? Or another one? An I, was it? Do you remember that, the I? Or a U?>

[Silence]

<Then what happened?>

On the way I ... I lost it.

<All right, then. Where did you lose it? Do you remember where you lost it?

You said you saw someone pick it up. That's what you told the officer. Who was it? Who picked it up? Did you recognise that person? Do you know them? Was it your love? Well, was it?>

Wasn't me, wasn't me, wasn't me!

[The interviewee, highly agitated, points accusingly at each person seated around the table, muttering all the while. Before the guards can apply an appropriate measure of restraint, the unit lurches to its feet and shouts <It was you!> with fury at the last person, then makes a half-hearted attempt to lunge across the table, arms outstretched, hands clawing the air. Having failed to assault any of the members of the interview panel, the unit slumps back into its chair, sobbing pathetically.]

Lost it, lost it.

[The other participants show no sign that anything is amiss.]

Report Template

The case is not closed; rather, it is on hold. It remains true, whether or not the unit "lost it", that it tried to resort to violence and refused to tell the truth. It was obvious to all that the letter was an unwarranted attempt at communication. Conclusion: The unit in question is too criminally inclined/ ruthless/evil/witless to say what the contents of the letter were.[68] It is also conceivable that the letter was not considered by the unit as an attempt at communication, but rather as a trinket, a fetish or a plaything. Whichever it is, the unit's actions are a violation of the Code, undermining the very basis of its existence, and must be dealt with accordingly.

However regrettable it may be for the unit to re-embrace past burdens and accept responsibility for them, it must speak any letters necessary for the full and optimal resolution of its case. Any attempt to resist or otherwise fail to do so will be reflected in the benefit term.

The clip is shown to trustees in training, followed by a quiz involving the above elements, to instil a deeper understanding of the issues involved and the appropriate constitutional responses.

Manifesto for Trustees: Creating Power, Freedom, Full Self-expression

1. Believe in the AlphaCode
2. We vow to continue today, tomorrow, forever
3. Our creative solutions work for all
4. Letters = needs
5. The Syntax is future, the future is Syntax
6. Redefine what is possible

68 Delete as necessary.

7. Words are worth the letters you have
8. The system cannot fail
9. No regrets ever
10. Never doubt the AlphaCode

•

Treatise #2, Ultra-level Associates

Call it what you will: the Fall, the Calamity, The Hardship, the Descent – out of that dark and desperate time of privation and chaos emerged the AlphaCode, which provided us with a once-in-a-lifetime opportunity to change society for the better. It required steely resolve and a degree of ruthlessness but it had to be done. And, let's not pretend otherwise, we were up for it! The advantages of ridding ourselves of the weak, the poor, the stupid, the old, and all those others deemed surplus to requirements, were obvious – a no-brainer, really. Essentially, we realised we had to rid ourselves of what became known as "the rottenest apples in society's barrel": the leeches, the parasites, the current and future would-be benefit cheats, those who are always mouthing off and demanding more, more, more of our precious resources while proffering nothing but insults in return. Did we care what became of them? No. Just so long as we didn't have to see them. Or, more to the point, hear them.

To the outsider, the approach we took may seems fragmented, but it's actually fully integrated, necessarily so. From the provision of dedicated purpose-designed spaces known as Central House/s to the scripted training briefs, everything works harmoniously and super-efficiently. Of course, without taking account of the wider context of communication and modern language use, our work would risk being only partially useful or, worse still, irrelevant. But from point-of-delivery to the units at ground level, all the way up to the thinktanks and research undertaken for future developments, our success is apparent and guaranteed future-perfect. We are, of course, aware of the naysayers and malcontents seeking to undermine our system of benefit by calling it – ludicrously, misleadingly – an Alphabet Tax. We will never publicly acknowledge this title, though it is true that the alphabet is at the heart of the Conversion and where our best work has been done. Our main concern is with the utilisation of individual letters and the strain our recipients, the Gifted, have in using them, from those unfortunates known as "full-handers", who still have a long way to go in the system to receive maximum support, to those far advanced in the system who are in receipt of the ultimate level of support and are, in other words, in complete recovery.

Words, a commodity of inestimable value, are now marketed and traded fairly and properly. It is, without doubt, an historic achievement, one that will cause future generations to scratch their heads, puzzled as to why this situation had remained so unsatisfactory for so long prior to our intervention, given that this delay produced outcomes that were nothing short of catastrophic.

•

Handling Currency – internal memo, n.d.

We have to admit to an error. We had been thoughtless, blind to the possibilities of language as currency: how it could be used in writing and speech, how much value it had, how it could be regulated, held in trust. We had to respond to this raft of possibilities effectively and generously. This was in addition to our other duties, the scope of which seemed endless, but whose weight we willingly bore, knowing that the units needed our help because they were unable to help themselves. We were and are answerable to all. Our obligation is to our entire domain.

But let's not dwell on the past! The work is now streamlined and moving in the right direction. We recognise that other responsibilities at letter level filter into the transformed word market, with mutually beneficial outcomes. The array of words that can no longer be used by the general public removes a further layer of difficulty for the Gifted, as does our letter benefit system. On another level entirely, once the ownership of words has been transferred, their handlers are at liberty to use this new material as they see fit.

We are aware, of course, that each transfer has the capacity to change the conditions of access. The outmoded term "copyright" is frequently invoked in this regard – usually to demonstrate its complete unfitness and to treat it with scorn. The two terms of which it is compounded are equally and separately dangerous: to copy is to steal, to indulge therefore in copywrong; and, let's be frank, no rights are accrued.

Like any commodity, words are regulated by the market. Rightly so. They're not free any more than speech is. To avoid unfortunate, wholly contradictory and inaccurate legacy connotations, we speak of "words" rather than "the word". "A word", by contrast, is entirely acceptable and indeed has gathered fresh meanings in the restored environment, pleasingly literal ones offering the suggestion of impending argument or conflict. There's no compulsion on the new handlers or, as some still say, "owners" of words to share freely, any more than there is on those who resources such as water or who control companies or other enterprises.[69] The situation for the Gifted, at whatever ben-

69 Note to self: **make sure this is re-edited**

efit level, has been further improved by the prohibition of certain obsolete or invalid parts of the vocabulary. Once withdrawn from circulation, the pressure to maintain them is lifted and the relief can be enormous.[70] In some quarters this has been described as "cancelled words". In effect, and on the whole, a wholly unbalanced load is deleted.

When the AlphaCode Conversion began its ministry with the idea of language as an integrated currency, some people misunderstood our intentions. Deliberately, I'd say. I'm not going to name names, but you know who I mean: those who think the worst of everyone and tend to see nothing but the bad in everything. I'm not talking about terrorists here – it's the normal, everyday, perpetually disgruntled contingent in our midst, the malcontents. It's as though they can't bring themselves to believe anything positive can happen or that anyone other than themselves is applying sufficient thought and effort to address the problem in question. Most likely their noses were put out of joint because they failed to come up with the solution first – because that's what we were doing, making sure, and I mean 100 per cent sure, that our chosen course of action was capable of delivering everything that was needed, a solution that worked to everyone's advantage. Everyone would get what they needed, thereby making their lives easier. Then, when everyone was more content and happier by far, they'd stop asking for more. Finally, best of all, they'd be quiet.

Thinking about it now (oh, the joy of hindsight!), it was probably the use of the word "currency" that caused the problem. Many meetings were spent discussing whether to use "commodity" rather than "currency". It's to be regretted that some people are terribly literal-minded and seem determined to undermine every little thing we do rather

70 Judging by reactions; anecdotally, according to valued trustees, indications of relief have included violence, shouting, crying.

than support our fine efforts. Although they're self-evidently wrong about almost everything, they blunder on, perpetually critical.

What these individuals fail to acknowledge is that "currency" is not just about dirty money and corruption, it contains layers of meaning. But they lack subtlety, and greater comprehension eludes them. That's the charitable view, anyway.

The truly important aspect of the meaning of currency is "the now". Currency represents nowness, the ever-modern, and it opens policy-attentive minds to the decisive futurity of our work. What possible objection could anyone have to that?

Sermon over, beg pardon!

•

Those fools, they deserved everything they got! Cameras everywhere, following their every movement – old-school surveillance, it's been around for decades, so they were used to it. And like the cameras that were broken half the time, or pointing in the wrong direction, or often weren't even switched on, our surveillance system was patchy at best. There was no sound recording at all, though we said there was. Not in so many words. Hints sufficed, just enough to induce a degree of paranoia. In fact, we didn't even bother to monitor their activities – why waste time and resources? Although the surveillance was all but non-existent, the units didn't know it. They believed we could hear their every word. They went quiet. From the kind and thoughtful <We Hear You> of the early days, to the get-you-in-the-neck alert, the units had been, shall we say, primed with the idea that we knew everything they said and did. Just the possibility that it might be true scared them into submission. Sweet.

•

Negative Elements – internal memo, n.d.

In order to reach this level of strategic and operational excellence, close attention had to be paid to the basic question of how best to satisfy the needs of each and every unit in receipt of the many grades of benefit, who are, after all, the reason why this Great Conversion has been undertaken. It's their manifold dependencies that have instigated the ongoing – indeed, our eternal commitment to the – development of the programme. Within the massive cohort of units, there are many stages and depths of need not responded to by numerous previous attempts at a system of benefits, attempts that were informed by so-called experts who proved incapable of thinking beyond the barricade of self-importance they'd erected between themselves and reality.

Huge amounts of time and money were wasted on their efforts, and although effort is required in all endeavours, achievement is what counts. That, sad to say, is precisely what was lacking. Although they claimed to be focusing exclusively on the units – which is what the Code is all about, after all – they made themselves the true focus of attention. Self self self, that's what it amounted to. But these self-appointed experts were wrong-headed from the very outset. They seemed convinced that there was nothing they didn't know, that any thought they had couldn't possibly be bettered, and that their ideas, stale though they were, would always succeed. That blinkered mindset is what we've worked tirelessly to overcome. But even having devised a programme as efficient in its delivery as the AlphaCode

Conversion, which is as nimble as can be in its adjustment to new circumstances and steadfast in its felicity to the welfare of the units, we do not self-aggrandise. It's enough to know that we were right and they were wrong.

Given the overwhelmingly positive nature of the AlphaCode at all stages from conception to delivery, it came as something of a surprise, and a far from pleasant one, to receive an inordinate amount of criticism, distrust and hostility from the selfsame self-proclaimed specialists we had expected to appreciate the value of our undertaking. They should have known and done better, but ... let's not dwell on the shortcomings of others; let's instead nudge their troublesome interventions to the margins where they may best be forgotten. We already knew not to listen to the carping of scientists, the social ones in particular. To everyone else bleating on about probity and specialist knowledge, we should have done the same. As it is, we had better things to get on with.

We spent a great deal of time on trying to improve the AlphaCode, and still do, even though improving a system universally acknowledged to be perfect is an impossible task. But the key difference between us and the carping know-it-alls is that our working lives are meaningful and valuable and theirs, quite obviously, are not.

Although the instigators of the AlphaCode Conversion were heavily criticised for it, they held to the early decision to make the system a free service. It remains so to this day. There were those who argued that recipients should be obliged to pay towards such an advantageous and generous multi-faceted benefit – an argument that won't be revisited because argument itself is redundant. Our response to the laughable "heritage" idea of "free" speech, as mentioned earlier, has been extended beyond the so-called "right" or "freedom" to articulate anything at all; it now embraces the concept of opinion, on anything, by anyone.[71] Having or expressing opinions or ideas or beliefs is now moot, an irrelevance. Indeed, it is now "mute", pardon the pun.

•

Retrieved Conference Paper – edit, n.d.

Don't get me wrong, we can shut them up. Yes, we can shut them all up. Shut them up and shut them down through the AlphaCode system of benefits. It's not just what they can articulate that's within our remit, the parameters of thought are defined too. By circumscribing thought, the range of action is thereby limited, and the concomitant reduction in vocabulary is pleasing because a reduction in possible responses limits time and reduces cost. Wins all round, I think.

This is a paradigm shift. Let me be clear: there are those whose language and available slots for talking had already been, it might be said, modest. We'd been working on it at all levels of educational provision through national and institutional curricula. It's no exaggeration to say that it had been a work in progress for many decades. It should also be acknowledged that what was achieved was never the complete solution. Frankly, the units still weren't quiet enough, and they didn't appreciate the massive raft of benefits by which so many aspects of their lives were improved.

It's different now. Everyone is quiet and treated the same. Ironically, it was the same treatment for all that the resistance groups were fighting for. It's what the struggle has ever been about: liberation for all. For which, a little appreciation from the units would be welcome, but that's not likely

71 Usual exceptions apply: "anyone" means other than us.

to happen. If they all stay quiet though, who cares!

Recovery, the total withdrawal of letters, is a time-consuming but eventual double-edged recovery of our resources. We don't have to pour resources into benefits and associated schemes to bring people to the acme of achievement; and, above all, we don't have to listen to them anymore, not ever. At the same time, Delites, as I think they call themselves (what nonsense!), or Gifted, or whatever we're supposed to call them now, achieve the joy of silence, blissful silence.

7. PostCode Accounts

In the final selection of witness accounts compiled by us archive folk, we reflect on the PostCode world with a series of memories, thoughts and speculations. Hindsight provides new perspectives on what happened, and even – given how quickly and how far we've come since the demise of ATax – what future steps to take, if need be. After the Code, what now?

We start with comments about the beginning of the end, when the Code began to disintegrate and life began to change for the better. We offer a panorama of pasts from this terrible, terrifying era from which we have only recently emerged. Here are contributions from people in many walks of life, including – controversially, for some – those who, at the lower levels, were complicit with or even supportive of the Code. But although change is possible for many of us, for some it's too soon, too painful. They can't bear to think about change because it forces them to dwell on the horrors they experienced under the Taxer regime. But although individual sensitivities must be respected, as a society we have to move on. Soon the archive group will present various ways and means by which our fractured society may be healed.

A number of Wall-Es have agreed to end their period of service by starting on a process of listening and recording. Really listening! Not just some pretence of listening, like the Coders scared us with. We want to reclaim their skewed slogan and make it mean what it should mean: We Hear You! Simultaneously, another cohort will be raised to the skills level and understanding required to continue this vital work. At which point the Wall-Es will step down and fade away. Because of the possibility of reprisals, many of our interviewees and contributors have chosen to remain anon. It's precautionary. But whether they choose to be identified or not, their words will help us to understand why things were as they were.

We are taking back control, and many hard decisions have to be made for the common good. For example, some AlphaCode terminology has been deemed unsalvageable. "Recovery", "conversion", "benefit", "syntax" – these words can no longer be used safely. It's probable that they'll always conjure up that oppressive time and reactivate painful memories. Anyone who continues to use them may be charged with a hate crime and/or verbal assault. While this may seem draconian, it's for everyone's safety and in all our best interests going, as they say, forward.

Testimony: MD

I'm dead to them, at least I hope so. I didn't really know what I was doing. It's true, I didn't. But I thought that if I push it and push it and get myself sent over the edge – wherever and whatever that is – I might be able to see something other people hadn't been able to see. I'd find out what was really going on. Then maybe I could do something about it, or at least tell other people so they could do something. Total madness! Talk about putting yourself on the line.

I'm no marvel, no hero. But it didn't go completely wrong for me. I was lucky; I did what I did when the Taxer regime was starting to crumble. And they knew it. Most of them, anyway. I was already down the tunnel by then, and when I saw the people in there, shock isn't in it. I thought: I'm going to die, and not prettily. Judging by the wretched state of the others down there, I didn't think they'd last long. Nor would I. And soon, like them, I'd wish I were dead.

Here's what I thought at the time: AlphaCode is done, likewise the Taxmen – the jailers and benefit police, anyway. Watchers, too. Then I began to think I'm kidding myself, I'll never get out, and even if I do we'll never get over what's been done to us. But I was right about the AlphaCode going down. The high-level Taxers, well, turns out they'd taken themselves off weeks before. They knew what was coming before anyone else did. Too late for those in the tunnels, though. Many of them had given up hope and believed that life above ground would be no better than where they were.

•

Testimony: Martha Hayward

First I think I must be ill. (I keep saying I I I me me me, because I can. Got it back, all back!) Sometime soon I hope we'll all get used to it, start using it again. So, yes, when I first see it, I think I'm dreaming ... or dying. Got to be a bit ill, surely. Hallucinating. Maybe it's just that I need to eat or sleep, or sit still until my head stops spinning. Shut my eyes and breathe deeply. It isn't the first time this has happened. I try to ignore it. Don't want to admit what I'm seeing. Don't want trouble. It's pointless; we're never going to get back to where we were before the shutdown. They wanted us quiet for good, so kept us busy saving our letters. All the time thinking about how we could say more with less, which of course we couldn't. Completely futile. No wonder we just gave up. But I couldn't ignore what I saw, or thought I saw, once I'd run through all the excuses that would let me avoid any trouble. And it's true, I can't see very well. Food, age, lighting, vitamins – who knows what the problem is. So the first few times, I don't think it amounts to anything. Don't know about the changes that are occurring. Maybe I just piece it together one day because I've taken the right route to Central and seen the letters on the wall. Yes, really, writing on a wall. Maybe I just see things better that day. Dunno.

Yes yes, all right, I'm getting to it. Don't rush me. Still part of me that holds the fear close. To be safe you learn to say nothing. Always having to keep your mouth shut. I don't think that'll go away for a very long time.

So I may be going crazy, seeing things, you know? Someone sending me a message kinda thing. Sounds loopy, doesn't it? Someone reaching out to me from the great beyond, woo woo. Just some letters, that's all I see. Nothing I can make sense of. Nought. Zero. 0 0 0. Letters are everything but had been reduced to nothing. They were once our lifeblood, air, water, whatever. Necessary for survival. Essential to live life to the full. There were signs and systems, looks and touch, yeah yeah yeah. All of that. But look at it this way: if they aren't worth anything, those letters, all that talk, why take them off us? Why build a massive system for just that purpose? Did they really go to all that trouble just to keep us quiet?

What I see are letters. Druggie? Am I? Ha, maybe. If only. Letters – that's what I'm desperate to have. It's a fantasy based on my deepest desires. That's what someone says it is, and it makes sense to me, kind of.

•

Testimony: KD

That time early on, outside Central, the tall one, the traffic island one. I forget a lot already by then, spelling stuff. Probably forget what some of them are, even. Y J K Q – they're the first to go. I know that now. And I, of course. But you always remember the I-word. If you forget that, it's over, you're finished. And the worst thing is, you have to struggle not to use it.

G O N E / O V E R

G A M E O V E R

One letter on a stone, that's what I see on the first occasion. The first time I remember, anyway. It was ages before it made any sense to me. Game over, all done. With the Tax, like.

Much later, once the Tax was on its way out, when you started seeing others, I met people who said they saw words, messages even, in some places. We swap stories. Some of them find ways to write it down, no idea how. Maybe they were Wall ones.

One of the Houses has been kept just as it was, so no one can forget. Frozen in time. But there's a bookshop one – imagine that! A public library or two, though with hardly any books. Some are now schools. Makes me cry, almost. There's a list of ideas you can add to. But no houses! That won't happen anyway, because who'd want to live there? Be more like a cemetery. Probably is. There's sure to be a body or two still undiscovered at the foot of some slippery staircase, or maybe under a trapdoor, don't you reckon?

•

Testimony: anon

It's because you learn to walk that way. You want to see what's coming – be warned, take precautions, yes. But looking straight ahead, that's not a good way to do it. You want to keep your eye on what might be kicking off, what you might have to avoid. Keep your eye on the ball. So you look down. If you look straight ahead, head held high, it's like you've got a right to be walking that way, taking up space, seeing the sights, even. And that's not for the likes of us. Look down. Then, when you glance up – beautiful sky, see that bird, where's that music coming from, look at the bridge. Well, in your dreams. Like you've got all the time in the world to see the world. Like you're actually there to enjoy life.

So you look down, needing to check your footing. If you haven't got that safe and secure, you'll take a tumble. Not worth risking it. So that's it: you have to look down. But you also have to glance up now and then, keep checking in that way too. It gets to be automatic. It's what you have to do. One or two need to be told that, but most people just do it automatically. When you look up, you see there's a lot missing – the trees, all that. Those scriptors, noters – what do you call them? Wall-Es? Anyway, the people putting the letters out; they know how Alfabs are always looking down. They must have thought about finding places where we'd see the letters. And not just down, on the pavements; places where only us Alfabs would go.

G I F T E D? N O – T A X E D

A L FA Bs R U S – W A L K T H I S W A Y

A L FA Bs U S U ME WE NOT T H E M

TAX IS OUT

~~CENTRAL HOUSE~~ ALL CLEAR
And a picture of a bright red feather with an X through it.

ALL YOURS

FULL HAND HERE

NO MORE BENEFIT

MORE LETTERS

NO MORE CODE

That day I see it, big and bold. I think I've died again, or I'm going to. Like I've been hit really hard and my eyes have gone funny, all colours, wobbly and freezing, rainbows and bubbles, you remember? Every which way, totally wha-a-a-t?? The end of the world. Or the beginning.

•

Testimony: Anon, Wall-E

When I notice it, it's scratches, holes. Like that. Stuff fallen off, taken away. That's what I think. Bits missing. I say I notice, but really I don't. I mean, what's there to see? Nothing's going on, nothing unusual or different. It's what it's like all the time. Stuff missing, broken things. There's no one to do repairs or make do. Everything is left to fall apart, get worse, turn to rubble and dust. And how it looks is how it is, how life is supposed to be. Not accidental.

Unforeseen, unanticipated advantages, you say? What a mouthful! What's that supposed to mean, advantages? Not sure I get it. But maybe, yes, it's possible. You see it around you, you feel it inside yourself; it matches, makes sense. Kind of confirms it somehow. Adds weight to it. As if this is how things are supposed to be. Like it's obvious and makes sense. Am I making sense? Anyway, I see a bit of splintered wood on a chair in Central, and it's shaped almost like a letter. C, it was. Am I getting obsessed, going a bit mad? Is it one of the Taxers having a larf? Har har, here you go, here's another letter for you. Makes you think, though. Makes you notice.

And after, when I come by again, some letters lighter, as usual, I remember what I saw. I look again, and yesss, there's another one, an A, capital one. Next time I go past, I walk around the chair without looking. I check to see no one is watching before I dare look. And yes! I see R and E. Easy that time, see it in order: C-A-R-E. Care. Is that an order, telling me what to do? And who made this word, where had it come from? The Coders? If so, what would that mean? Telling me that "care" exists, even in Central? But no idea whether it's from one of them or one of us.

We had one of them Coder rats in the Wall-Es. We were really careful, or thought we were. Keeping it hush-hush. Groups kept small, local, only people you know and think you can trust. One of them pretending to be one of us. Don't know which one, to this day. You hear rumours that if they flip sides, go native – and it does happen – down the wrong lift they go, through the trapdoor sharpish. Sorry, shouldn't joke about it. But I'm not laughing either.

•

Testimony: Jan Davis, Wall-E

Someone's having a laugh, I think, when I first see it. Nice idea; that simple. A little message. Who knows where it came from or who was behind it. But the letters outside kept coming. Or maybe it's that I'd started looking for them. Then I began to see more and more. Wondered if I was overdoing something, having a funny turn. Suddenly they were all over the place: when I look down at the pavement; when I look up. I saw them even when I was in the tunnels. They never say much, and when I went back to the same place the following day, what I saw wasn't there anymore. Even in Central I saw them. Yes, really! There's a

H I
or a
S T E P
and a
D R O P
or
D A R K

– like warnings to help you. Sometimes written in chalky stuff, like flour. But then I thought, who'd waste scant resources on that? Sometimes the letters were laid out using slices of fruit or tiny bits of peel. Then you'd want to eat and read, all at the same time. You wondered: What would feed you the most, words or food? Or sometimes the letters looked like they were written in soot. In the tunnels I saw letters made of white stuff, too, so you'd be better able to see them because it's well dingy down there. Mud – I saw that used a few times too, crafted to make the letters stand out from the wall. And sometimes the letters looked like they'd been dug out with something sharp and hard. Either way, you noticed.

T A L K

K E E P G O I N G

Anyone who sees it, needs it. Glad of it. Keeps you going, it really does. Seeing letters, words, makes you know someone's trying; it makes you dare to try to talk, to keep on trying. Everyone has those times. More and more often it happens with me. Then I start to think: can't be bothered anymore, too tired, too scared. Best keep quiet. I can't be the only one who thinks like that. If you're lucky, if you're ok, and if you have the letters, well, of course you come back, I mean come back to thinking "No, I won't be quiet, I won't shut up. And I won't let the others get shut up either. You be quiet, you Taxers. Not us." If we stop talking or stop trying to talk, that's it, they win. So keep going, please! Don't give up! Terrorists, the Taxers call us, because we act like there's another way, which there is. We keep people in practice, so they keep trying – that's the important thing.

•

Testimony: John Towne

I keep shutting my eyes to start with. Then rubbing them, blinking. This can't be happening, not even in dreams. No one talks about dreams anymore in case a watchman hears or the recording picks it up. Or a squealer – and God alone knows who they are. Any which way, it's too frightening. Does everyone think the same about this? Never ask. That's too frightening too. If they're good dreams, and you have to wake up, it's hard. If they're bad, not so much, even though there's nothing good to wake up to. But sometimes it's a good one, a dream you never want to wake up from. Wouldn't it be nice to stay asleep forever? And once you've had that thought, it's hard to turn it off. Hard to come back from there, to make peace with what's here, without hope of anything else.

It's funny, yeah. When did I last laugh like that? So funny and scary. So frightened. You don't know what anyone else can see. Everyone is really quiet about it. About everything, really. Scared? Yes, that too. I get hot and red in the face. And hot all over, like, shooting up, whoosh, toe to head. Think I might keel over. All done, too much, like a thunderclap inside. Doesn't seem like a bad way to go. A bang, a smash out, a blast off – not a wail or a whimper. Did it go through my head at the time? Who knows, there's too much, all of it loud and busy. Excited – terrified, really. What's going on, what does it mean, where can I go, what can I say? Yes, what can I say? Not much left to say, that's the thing. Can I shout? How much have I got left to say? Too soon to think it's the end of anything, too big a hope. Never think I'll be around to see it. But maybe something different will happen, because difference can be better. Change comes along whether you like it or not. And maybe this is what change is like, what it can be.

It's not as if everything changes right away. Some of it happens quickly, though. Face unfreezes. Mouth shapes itself around words. Then it all goes backwards – wait a minute there, idiot, what do you think this is? Who told you to do this, that you can do this? Who said it was allowed? What are you, stupid? Learned nothing? That's me keeping me in check, out of my own head.

You can't imagine why they'd do that – keep all the evidence of what they did, I mean. Have to think it through, but not try to understand. I. D.O. N.O.T. W.A.N.T. T.O. U.N.D.E.R.S.T.A.N.D. Avoid empathy or forgiveness. They don't deserve it. They're not getting that from me, ever.

•

Testimony: PA

It's like a new way of being, a new life. Sounds silly, doesn't it? But everything opens up that way – takes you away from the down stuff, the downside of everything: the mud, the rubbish, the holes in the road, the greyness and bleakness. You start to see other things too. People ... sometimes they'd look out from windows, no one to tell them not to any more. Someone waves a hand, friendly like. Not the usual: "Get away from me!" A smile, a hint of one, from someone walking past. Wink of an eye? Just a twitch, maybe. But probably not. Whatever it is, it's a form of communication. And I wouldn't have seen it if I hadn't stopped looking down all the time. For a long time I had to keep telling myself to look up, look up, until I get used to it again.

The other stuff, the signs and messages ... maybe some of it was always there, in plain sight, but no one had the courage to look.

NEARLY THERE

"Where?" I think, first time I see it. ABCastle? Wish I wasn't anywhere near it. Wish I could turn around and go elsewhere. Wish I could. I don't want to get there, ever. But as there's nowhere else to go, I have to go. And go and go, whenever they say. But then, after leaving Central, going down the road, I see the sign again. It says

DON'T STOP

KEEP GOING

Sounds like a good idea. Immediately I feel less tired. Lively, almost. Alive, certainly.

Colours are different, I reckon. It all adds up. And then I get scared again. Who is doing this to me? What's going to happen now that I've seen this? They'll know I know. But nothing happens, and I start to like it more and more, it starts to feel like an old friend, and then I'm less scared. And not long after, around those times, you realise there isn't anyone to know what I think. I can know what I like, and there's no one at Central or anywhere else to stop me. And the messages get longer, like they're talking to me. I know it sounds stupid. But I'm not mad; it's like that, really. Almost like a chat between me and whoever or whatever it is. I'm not talking back, though – thinking back, maybe. Talking back in my head. Then there's another message, and it all starts to add up. That's how I see it, anyway.

SOON ALL OVER

DIFFERENT AGAIN

NOT LONG NOW BETTER TIMES

It could be about anything, in a way. You make of it what you will. Maybe that's what it's for, showing the way to the get-out.

•

Testimony: SD

I've been in Central for ... hours it feels like. Do this do that go there – no, you idiot, there! Up those stairs, along that corridor, through that door, and that one, and no, not in here, and you're late again. Let's increase your benefit again – that'll help. Release you from another four. So I was down to a three-hander. And this is early on, after the first Big Quiet, as they called it. Most times you just do what you're told. Don't think, just react. That's what you learn. Have to. If you don't, you're really in trouble. Just get over it and get out as soon as you can. But one day, I don't get over it. I'm not broken, just angry. Then there he was. Never seen anyone there before. Never seen him, either, here or anywhere else. So I spew the anger out in front of him and stomp off. Don't know why. To get safely home, I suppose. I was worried about what I'd just done. Later on, he said he could see the steam rising off me. That was much later, when we knew we could both be trusted.

When I cooled down, I got proper scared. Must have been well gone or I wouldn't have said a word, not to someone I don't know. You must be bloody mad, I thought. I was talking to myself, loosening my lip. Didn't know I still could. "So," I said, "who's that squealer and what have I gone and done now, telling him that." That could've been it for me. For days I worried about what I'd said. Worried about saying anything at all. Wondered whether I could make out I was talking about something else? But you know it won't matter in the end; I shouldn't have been talking at all. No defence, all offence – that's how it works. If you get reported, that's it, you're done.

Don't know how long it was before I saw him again, outside Central. He says he kept going past, but not so often that they'd notice. We talked some more. Him, mostly. He may have stuff on me, but now I've got stuff on him too. It works both ways. We don't have to trust each other, but we're in the same boat.

And it keeps on happening. I say a bit more and he says more too. Slowly, at first, until we get to ... well, "What can we do about any of this?" It isn't like we think the same about everything. We haven't come from the same place. That was another way they get you where they want you: there's not enough common ground. Everyone is too damaged to make common cause. Then they tip us into the so-called Big Quiet, and here we all are, shut up and shut down for good. Can't even think. So we sit it out, keep schtum. No fight left in us. We all have our own wounds to lick, don't want to lick anyone else's. But there's just enough between us right then to talk about it. For me, it's like a test. Then, next time, it's not him, the one I've talked to, it's another one – a woman. And you wonder: What is it they're after?

•

Testimony: Henry Bryant

Once, one time, I come here and see someone, another Delite, can tell straight away by look alone. So many times and I've never seen another. That time, the route took me a different way, so I saw other halls and passages, but then they do all tend to look the same. Except this time there was something I'd never seen before: a roomful of machinery. Quiet, idle. Each of them had a round metal drum as part of it, but that was the only similarity. Paper with letters on the floor, letters in a row, starting ABC. And that scared me, because I knew that wasn't allowed anymore. It must have been a mistake for me to go that way, a power-out or a programme malfunction. Can that even happen? The machines were in a space on the floor below me. It was like their ceiling had been cut out, or part of my floor, to make a double-height space. What I was on was a kind of viewing platform, and I hate to think who or what they had in mind when they made that. Had they bred different to us? Were there massive robots working the machines? Had the Coders become a race of giants? That's a joke, by the way, in case you've lost your sense of humour. I walked the whole way round, looking down all the while, taking as long as it took. No prods, no messages, no clicks – nothing. Nothing happened. That's when I knew how far gone the whole thing was. It was like I'd got away with something. Then I knew, it was over.

•

Anon, Coder Admission Statement

And you start to wonder: how deep does it go? Are we all labouring under strictures that are more or less comprehensible, more or less tacitly acknowledged, or deeply embedded and camouflaged? Does it sound too paranoid, too conspiracy theorist to wonder if it's all part of the same system, always right as an idea and a procedural principle from inception, planned to be this way? Envisaged as an international system rather than one that affected only the Deliterati? And what a Delite they are! (There, I've said it. Something has really shifted if I'm daring to put something like that into words.) Not their fault, I know. What was The Hardship about, anyway? I mean, really about? I'm too young to know. My mum, she was on the watch, then a trustee. Now me.

After they brought in the Big Quiet, only us Coders were allowed to speak. Which makes perfect sense, because only what we had to say was of value. It's a system whereby each layer of people knows what their own layer knows, and that's it. The other layers don't know about your layer and you don't know about theirs. And given what the whole restrictive system is about, they can rely on other people's communication to stay put, not cross between layers, neither up nor down. And why is that? Because it might cause confusion. Looking back, I can see we got a bit giddy. There was that letter calculator software we said had been developed by one of our world-beating engineers. It was supposed to be able to hear and quantify the number of letters the unit was using, and, what's more, identify which unit had been speaking because of its unique voiceprint. Nonsense, of course, but news of it spread fast and those poor fools bought it. They really thought we had all this data at Central House/s for their assessments. So stupid! – they deserved everything they got. No no, sorry, shouldn't say that. I forgot myself for a moment.

We thought we were above it all because we were delivering it, right? We imagined that none of it was being done to us, that we were only doing it to them. That's the word: imagined. I can see that now, and I'm genuinely sorry.

•

Testimony: SH

"We Hear You" – you saw that slogan plastered everywhere, on the front and back of buildings, by the roadside, on posters. It was around the time The Hardship ended and the Big Quiet began, if I remember it right. And first off some of us thought: Uh-oh, here we go, another "We're all in it together" moment. Yeah, yeah. But now, with this new version, we were desperate for something. Not sure what.

How desperate we must have been to take even a smidgen of comfort from some old nonsense like that, and from them. "We

Hear You" – makes me puke now just to think of it. They made it look right, though: the colours, the cut of the letters, the pictures behind the words. So there was something reassuring about it, and it worked. We thought the Coders or Conversionists or whatever they called themselves back then were on our side. It was comforting to see pictures of people who looked a bit like us, like we used to look before everyone was hungry and dirty.

•

Testimony: AF

Red feather – that was their signal: Stop right there! I don't know how they knew when our rations were used up. Or even if they did know. It went quiet in your mind and you clammed up. The red feather showed that your letters had run out, shelf life over, sell-by date past, and no "still fresh" indicator. Reassessment due. You had to go back to Central House. A prompt. A warning. Something like that. The red feather showed you'd somehow got it wrong, you'd mismanaged your letters. And when you get it wrong, and you will, that'll be your fault, no one else's. Or if you don't get it wrong, that'll be your fault too.

"Recovery" they call it, but for us it wasn't like getting your health or anything else back. Nothing ever came back or got better. Then the feather would arrive. Every time it would appear right in front of you, no idea how. You couldn't miss it, and they'd know you must have seen it, lying on the road as it was, or stuck to a wall. "Knock you down with a feather" – isn't that what people used to say?

They can send out all the statements they want. What's owed, what allowance, what cut, what benefit – what's the use? There's the red one, and then recovery means you're done, it's finished, all better. Not an ounce of sense to it. Tell me different, if you can.

•

Testimony: Daniel Howard

The initial shock was so powerful, such an intense blow, that what came after barely registered. So there was no comeback, no debate. Telling me I can talk only sparingly, using these few letters. The incremental damage was massive but it came in relatively small stages. Everyone was still reeling from the Big One, no matter what they believed. Usually they'd say they were "speechless". But that's not funny, in this case.

Not only were we shocked into silence, we were ordered into it. No, that's not funny either. But we were. By the time we'd picked ourselves up from the shock, we were further down the road towards the Quiet. When I say "we", I mean me. Don't know if that was true of everyone. That's what it looked like and sounded like to me. We were picking ourselves up and starting over, except there was very little left to start with. Every time we woke up or turned around it felt like there was less and less to get going with. Every time we opened our mouths there was less that was able to come out.

•

Testimony: CG

You want to know which letters are the most sought after, the most valued? Are any letters sacred, even? Some are clearly taboo, as in unsayable. People struggle now to get A and C out of their mouths. No Xs anymore. Everyone has favourites, though. Some people swear they can't manage without an E – there's plenty of them about. Or used to be. The people, not the letter. You'd hear them when the waiting rooms were still there. They should get together and make a party of it. Then there are those who like it because it's E one way up, or an M or two Ns when turned clockwise, or even, if you turn it more, a W. They're the ones who like shapes. They go for an S, too, or the old Z, but almost no one has had that for ages.

I wouldn't say this to many people, but with the Z what they did makes sense. I mean, really, what's the point of it? I think they're right: it's a waste of time and resources. But I keep my opinion to myself. And the K and the J, come to that. What the Taxers did still has an essential newness, despite having been done so many years ago. It's never lost that innovative thrust, I'll give them that. Sorry.

Y it was, for her. And U and R. But that was our secret. Only mine now. She could certainly use it (who couldn't?). It says it all: that's what I wanted to say, and there's no quicker way to say it. Plenty go for the O – multipurpose, see. O or 0 – really, who cares about that anymore? Yes, if you're going to be all back-in-the-dayish; it's not the same, but that's how everyone uses it. O as in Oh. It's surprise, pain, fear. Even wonder and pleasure, if that's back too.

Nah, Xs don't do it for anyone no more. Everyone's got them, so who cares? If that's all you've got, it's the last chance saloon. So X can't be considered any kind of prize. Cheap as chips and always was. Just as well, too. In big demand when all those poor souls can't use anything else, when it's the only mark they can make. The A, I'm going to say, overall. Is that what everyone says? L? You're kidding me. What's that about, then? Oh, ok, like O then ... Or could be a number. Looks like a small el or capital i or even a one. Simple, strong, straight. But as for A, you can't fault it, it's the beginning of everything. Start me up. Climb up those solid sides – an A frame, see, sturdy, simple again. Or the other ways how it looks, little or large. Can't go far without it.

What else? There's not many more, really. Not in our pockets. And those with the most aren't going to feel fond about any of them; it was just normal, what they got. Now that all 26 letters are back, we don't know what to do with them.

It's hard, though, having to keep away from A. Everyone wants the As and Zs, it's the old AtoZ, the ABC. They might not remember but they know it used to mean something. AtoZ, how to get every-where, anywhere you want to go. A to B and back again. Not that that will get you very far. Everyone wants to start at the very beginning. It's a very good place, innit? Or was. Have to start somewhere else now. A's had its day. Time for new beginnings. We'll have to work out what that means.

<That'll keep them quiet.> Ha! <That'll shut them right up.> What do they know? Qs are easy. Ps, I'll work out how my mouth makes it and, ah, Bs. That's it. Bs'll do it, near enough. Keep 'em! you want them? Got big Fs to fry, me. You watch your Ps and Qs, young man.

Here's a little song I made up, for in my head like.
>   Take away my D-I-V …
>   If you want a J-O-B
>   -O R S. That's the end of us. There's no coming back from it.
>   I've got no R-E-S-P …
>   E-C?
>   Or any R-C-E-S
>   Not my IOU, and not my Es, that's not funny!
>   The r-e-s-t, it's yours to keep.

•

Testimony: E Spencer

Then one day the red feathers stopped coming. Sometimes you'd "overspent" – overspoke, really – and they'd come quickly, even in quiet months when you were watching your mouth. You knew that if there was a mistake it would always be yours, never theirs. But someone must have flicked a switch or pulled a lever or whatever: suddenly, no more feathers. That's when people started talking again, and they got away with it. You had to ask yourself: Is no one noticing?

I go to Central at the time they said to go, the correct time, ten minutes early, and find it's closed. Doesn't look any different from usual, no more shut than it always looks. But you can't get in, and soon enough others turn up who can't get in either. First time almost that you see anyone else there. You know they're there, right enough. You might even hear a step, a shout. But usually you won't see another of your own kind. That's when it gets real scary. Fear time, I'm telling you. Central House closed?! What can that possibly mean? So we walk to the next one. And the next, and the next, and we keep going to every Central House that anyone knows of, until we realise we've visited them all, every single bloody one of them. All shut.

There's a lot of them to get around, too, and a lot of us doing it by then. Like a hunger march – you seen the old photos? Everyone keeps saying they didn't realise there were so many Centrals. To be honest, it's terrifying not knowing what's happening, but also, because we're so scared, we aren't joyful together, not at first. Some people start to sing as we walk. Wordless singing. But it doesn't take. Some still won't speak, too frightened in case they say one word too many and they'll cop it when Central House opens again. There are fights too, out of fear mainly and sheer disbelief. Mistrust. No solidarity. None of us know what's what anymore. A couple of times, people think they've spotted a red feather, and it's like they're almost relieved, you can tell. Not pleased, but relieved. Like back to normal, phew, the good old bad old days. And anyway, even if they had spotted one, how could you tell whose it was? But how did we ever? Mine! Saw it first! Ha-bloody-ha!

•

Testimony: TH

I'm a believer. They keep repeating their mantra and I keep believing. I think: Right, that's the way to go. Just what's needed. Fair and square. To each what they deserve. What you put in is what you get out. Yes, and why wouldn't you think that?

I know it's going to be hard. It'll take some getting used to. Tough solutions to tough problems. We need to get back on track, stop wasting everything on them that don't put anything back, only take, because ... well, because they can get away with it. And who are "they"? Don't matter, does it? Them that don't share the same values as us. Outsiders. It's different if you come from over there; bound to be. Can't blame them, I suppose. Well, you can. I did. Thought they ought to know better, come round to our way of thinking and do as we do. As they should, 'cos we're the best, always have been. Only reason we have these problems is because of them. We've been much too tolerant, too generous, too soft. We should chuck 'em all out, get shot of 'em and get it done quick. Everyone I know thinks that. Us first, us only – that's how it should be.

Makes sense. Tough love to get us back on track. We all have our bit to play. All in it together. It'll hurt us too for a while, but not like it does them. And we'll manage. For as long as it takes, we'll be all right. A fresh start. New page (whatever that means). Like after the war, they keep saying, and I keep believing their stuff. I wanted to do my bit. Wanted to be a watchman, in particular, but they didn't need any more of them. Kept my ears open anyway. More than a few of them others I passed on to the watchers for overdoing it with the letters. They wouldn't keep quiet. Just not right, that. Don't know why they got benefit at all, tbh.

We have these devices, that's how the info gets to us, streaming. I believe the info without really knowing what it's all about. But it's a matter of trust, innit. I'm doing the right thing, aren't I? Yeah, that's it. No doubt in my mind. I believe. I do. The kids, my kids, aren't onboard, though. We fall out over it, can't talk about it without getting into a bloody big row. They stop coming to visit, won't see me, and I won't let it go. I used to hear from them now and then, the kids, but not for a while now. No idea where they are or what's happened to them.

That was me. That's what I used to think.

•

Testimony: Jane Birch

They call it benefit but that doesn't make sense. It's not giving, it's taking away what's needed. Can't get more letters so can't make the words. Can't pay for more either, even if you had the money. Don't know where you go if they cut you right off, if you run out completely. They don't talk about what they take away, only what you get, what they're giving you: freedom. Without the letters, I dunno, it's hard to keep making what you had. Can't even talk about it – they'll hear you and it'll be on record. You'll get even less then. That's the point, yeah?

No, you can't talk about it; and even if you had enough letters, why would you try? It's too hard to keep thinking of new ways to use what little you've got left, and there's less and less that can be said. Too hard to keep struggling to make less and less be enough. It's like an off-switch, an unspeak button. What hurts is you kind of know you're doing it to yourself. That's the worst of it.

•

Testimony: Annie Blake

Not much left to say, really. Just accusations and resentments. "Never seems to shut her mouth, that one, but she's still got more letters than me. How come?" Always less, never more. Not talking now, even when we're not not talking – you get what I mean? To talk you have to have another person with letters like you, otherwise it just won't work. And maybe it hurts them to try to talk, them with only a handful of letters. Can talk "to" them but can't talk "with" them, so that's no good.

Bridge and tunnel people, though, they're the ones who can cross over any which way, between all. Dunno how they do all that passing. You can see who's got what, though. Dunno how. It used to be how people sounded, where they came from and how high up, but now you know from how they look. It's where you see them, what they're doing, how they're doing it. It's all of a piece.

That's what's so clever, see. I hate to say it. So many ways to stop people talking. With the Tax, I mean. Taking away the nuts and bolts of language. And then there's the sanctions, the listeners and watchers, the stupid feather business. Most of all it's the fear. I shut up out of fear. Don't say anything if there's even the slightest chance that it's going to be heard and create more problems – the ones I have already are bad enough. Life is bad, why make it worse? So I don't just stop to think before I speak, I stop speaking entirely.

•

Testimony: Anon

All right, then.

I can't talk to anyone else but I can still talk to myself. Don't watch me, though, then I can do it. As far as I know my thoughts are still my own. They can't get inside my head. Not yet, anyway. Or if they can, if they can really do that, then it's all over and nothing else matters.

I'll just carry on telling myself the story. That way, I know at least one person is listening. No choice but to listen to myself. Everyone's a storyteller, right? Everyone can take charge of their own story, making it, shaping it, keeping to it, rising above it, looking back on it, learning through hindsight. And what about now? It's still dark and dank and wretched. No colour, no light, nothing. Every sense feels closed off, wiped out. It's like everything's been turned off. There's no lift in life, it's all flat and dull, and that's on a good day.

Makes sense, though. At one time people believed in what's called free speech. There was this idea that everyone had the same right to speak, to have their voice heard no matter what they wanted to say. It wasn't strictly true, only worked for some: those of the right colour, right school, right gender, right on the money and in the money. Especially those in the money. That got completely turned around and inside out with the shutdown. Then another time, when they tell you you can say some things but not others – a stage or a platform for it. Then there's this benefit to help people do their best speak. Nobody thinks it's going to be them. Someone else will get the benefit. That's how it works.

You've only yourself to blame if you've done something wrong, and if that's the case then AlphaTax is the punishment. But the Coders say that what they're doing is a cure-all; it's good, they say, not bad. Yes, that's what they say, over and over again, and in the end there's nothing left to say. You get punished if you say different. And if you think like that, well, obviously there's something wrong with you. It's your own fault for not knowing what's good for you, in your own best interests, and for everyone else's best interests too, and for not believing them when they tell you the Alphabet Tax is good for you. Except they don't call it that. They're proper fierce about it. More like a faith to them. It's the one-and-only, the only way, the right way.

The tax is making things better for everyone – that's how they see it. Has to be done because of The Hardship. Plenty of people see through it, though, enough of them to dare call it what it is, a tax, taking away what's ours by right.

•

Testimony: Jacob Sykes

It used to be – <you must …> or <we need you to …> and if you don't <…>. Like a contract. Like it was something you'd acknowledged as fair and just. An agreement between equals. But it wasn't like that, not at all. Whatever they tell you to do, you do it, or else. And "or else" is the nub of it, the tax, no ifs or buts, no going back. Or forward, really. <Free yourself. Unlearn that language. Open up to new opps. A radical, daring shift to new possibilities. It's a gift, a giving.> So they kept saying.

There's no appeal, no mistakes or forgetfulness allowed, no sickness, no special circs. Half the time people manage to keep to the agreement, but the terms or the times still get changed without them letting you know. You're always in the wrong, never them. You take the fall, or your letters do, no matter what.

When the techies came round to fix the recorders, it changed everything. They told us not to touch the recorders OR ELSE! It was our place, but it wasn't anymore. Not even the bedroom. Always and forever ours, we thought, but it turned out the Conversion was changing that too. At Central House they say it's like when we were <freed from the burden of the apostrophe and who noticed the difference then?> No idea what they're on about, but I suppose they mean it's to help people. After all, that's what it's supposed to be for. That's how they put it, anyway. So of course you don't believe them. Right from the off you know they're trying to put one over on you. Always on and on about the greengrocers and apples (you remember apples, don't you?). But greengrocers – what's that? Really, what's that about? Sometimes you wish they'd shut up, but that would be a stupid thing to wish for, wouldn't it?

•

Testimony: CW

Back in the day they stopped at 140 letters (imagine that, 140! – what an incredibly large number and what glorious days they were), and we also had the likey-like. You know: click, done, scroll. Had smiley faces too. That's bad for the planet, they said, bad for us. Too much hatey-hate for them, more like.

They tolerated it for a while, but not for long. Too much open and free communicado going on, letting us know where like-minded people could meet. But then too many riots, and harsh winters didn't keep the protesters indoors. They came out on the streets anyway and rioted to keep warm. Blocked the roads to stop cities working. Vandalised everything they could lay their hands on. Year after year that happened. But every year, when the hot summers came, protest fizzled out in the heat of the sun. The rioters, worn out, exhausted really, gave up what they'd been doing to stand in the sea and cool down. By then there was nothing to smiley-face about.

•

Testimony: Ed Baines

Say the wrong thing, say too much too often, and you'll end up in the tunnels before you've had time to blink. The tunnels, or wherever the so-called "recovery place" is that people don't come back from because, you know, they're having such a lovely time. That's what the Coders said. Time of their lives, they said. Oh, sure. So you shut yourself up, see! You keep schtum no matter how many letters you've got. They put the groundwork in, oh yes. But then people start doing it to themselves, drawing inward, keeping quiet, doing their job for them.

And this I should mention ... At Central, the one down by the river, there are trees, real ones with pale green leaves. One big one especially. I always notice it. And when I come out of Central that time, I see a smile had been carved into the trunk at eye level. It was really hard not to cry when I saw it. Didn't know I could still do that – cry, I mean. I swear, the smile wasn't there when I went in, just a few minutes earlier. I don't really know what to think, but because no one could have seen it before I did, I think, well, maybe it's a message for me. But who from?

I know that's the kind of thing you want to hear, and I'm trying to tell you. You've got to be patient. Going there in my mind to tell you about it, it hurts. And the time's all mixed up. No, not like it was yesterday; it doesn't feel like that, not quite. But not as long as a year ago. I stiffen when I think about it. My muscles and brain seize up and I feel really, really tired. Everything achy and heavy. I said I'd tell my story and I'm trying to, but everything hurts, so be patient.

•

Testimony: RA

Who turned the lights off? Who was last to leave? We simply don't know. There must still be people around who know everything, but no one's come out of the woodwork yet and we've no idea where they went. Perhaps they didn't actually run to the exit, just changed their clothes and strolled out of Central House/s, casual like. Gone to a safe haven somewhere. As for the bodies in the tunnels, you can tell they're not Coders. That lot look very different from those they call the recovered. If they were Coders, the bodies would be fully dressed, wearing decent shoes, and also, you know, they'd be well-nourished, still have all their own teeth. I could go on. There's still a lot for us to find out. Once the windows are open and the lighting's adjusted in CH#1 and the rest of them, it doesn't even look that strange. Just ordinary. Boring. Far from welcoming, though, which is what they wanted.

•

Testimony: Anon

That's how it started, the Code, with the "We're All In It Together" slogan. Harmless enough, helpful even. Then before you knew it, we found ourselves shut out, shut up. It might sound unbelievable to you, a made-up story even, but you wouldn't believe how fast the Code took hold, became what everyday life was like. New normal, they said, but what I'd thought was normal was really abnormal and I couldn't stand it anymore. There, I've said it. I admit, I used to be one of them, had the full hand, all 26. Said what I liked, as a Watcher, but then I saw the light and switched over, became a Wall-E.

Misinformation is how it began, bending the truth into unnatural shapes. Lies. Bigger and bigger ones. But more than that. As a Watcher, I saw it from the inside: a targeted, thought-out assault on everyone but themselves through policymaking that became ever more unscrupulous and cruel as the years went by. I get that not everyone thinks that way. There are those who think it just happened, that it was some kind of accident – started out as one thing but somehow turned into something else, malign, when they got the bit between their teeth, capitalising on their strengths. Good for you, if that's how you think.

Endnote

Now you know how it worked, easy as ABC. And here the story comes to the end of the Code, such as we've been able to piece it together so far. We all know what The Alphabet Tax cost us; now we have to get into the XYZ of how it began, how it stuck, to make sure it can never happen again. We're getting there; the archive is only the beginning. As you've read, some of our respondents already look to the future. Others prefer to work on disentangling the threads of what brought us here. To avoid a repetition of the misery, cruelties and social iniquities the Coders visited upon us – that they built around us – we must do both. Other people believe we should spend all our efforts on ways of forgetting. But one thing's for sure: the tax is over. This is where we are now. Are you ready for a new beginning?

Also available from grand**IOTA**

Brian Marley: APROPOS JIMMY INKLING
978-1-874400-73-8 318pp

Ken Edwards: WILD METRICS
978-1-874400-74-5 244pp

Fanny Howe: BRONTE WILDE
978-1-874400-75-2 158pp

Ken Edwards: THE GREY AREA
978-1-874400-76-9 328pp

Alan Singer: PLAY, A NOVEL
978-1-874400-77-6 268pp

Brian Marley: THE SHENANIGANS
978-1-874400-78-3 220pp

Barbara Guest: SEEKING AIR
978-1-874400-79-0 218pp

Toby Olson: JOURNEYS ON A DIME
978-1-874400-80-6 300pp

Philip Terry: BONE
978-1-874400-81-3 150pp

James Russell: GREATER LONDON: A NOVEL
978-1-874400-82-2 276pp

Askold Melnyczuk: THE MAN WHO WOULD NOT BOW
978-1-874400-83-7 196pp

Andrew Key: ROSS HALL
978-1-874400-84-4 190pp

Edmond Caldwell: HUMAN WISHES/ENEMY COMBATANT
978-1-874400-85-1 298pp

Ken Edwards: SECRET ORBIT
978-1-874400-86-8 254pp

Giles Goodland: OF DISCOURSE
978-1-874400-87-5 302pp

Production of this book has been made possible with the help of the following individuals and organisations who subscribed in advance:

Peter Bamfield
Christopher Beckett
Jan Blake-Harbord
Geoffrey Brackett
Paul Bream
Andrew Brewerton
Ian Brinton
Jasper Brinton
Peter Brown
Alison Burns
Emily Candela
Sue Cavanagh
Cris Cheek
Sue Cheetham
Sarah Cooper
Claire Crowther
Allen Fisher/Spanner
Miles Gibson
Daniel Green
Paul Griffiths
Penny Grossi
Charlie Hague
Randolph Healy
Jo Henderson
Jeremy Hilton
Gad Hollander
Peter Hughes
Robert Hughes
Kristoffer Jacobson
Andrew Key
Margaret Kitching
Sharon Kivland
Maria Lloyd

Richard Makin
Michael Mann
Sam May
Peter Middleton
Nicole Mollett
Paul Nightingale
John Olson
Toby Olson
Lucinda Oestreicher
Sean Pemberton
Frances Presley
Christopher Pusateri
David Rose
Lou Rowan
Emily Rubin
Dave Russell
James Russell
Ruth Sandbach
Geoff Sawers
Edward Sayeed
Hanne Scrase
Pablo Seoane
Alan Singer
Cedric Soertsz
Ulrike Steven
Eileen Tabios
Harriet Tarlo
Susan Tilley
visual associations
Sarah Watkinson
John Wilkinson
Eley Williams
Stamatis Zografos

www.grandiota.co.uk